KU-731-928

A MAN WITH A MAID 2

Following the 'exciting events' of the first volume of a *Man With A Maid* – in which the Victorian gentleman Jack wrought exquisite revenge on the 'maid' Alice in his specially constructed, sound proof room – Jack once more plans adventures of a saucy nature. In issuing an invitation to Alice's haughty sister Marion 'as you shall see, a whole new sequence of the most thrilling and lascivious events was destined to take place in the privacy of my little harem, my torture chamber, my bordello deluxe . . . namely, my Snuggery!'

Also available in Nexus Books

A MAN WITH A MAID 1
A MAN WITH A MAID 3

A MAN WITH A MAID 2

Anonymous

This edition first published in 1993
by Nexus Books
338 Ladbroke Grove
London W10 5AH
First published in Great Britain 1982
Reprinted 1982, 1983, 1984, 1985, 1987, 1988, 1989

Printed and bound in Great Britain by
Cox & Wyman Ltd, Reading, Berkshire

Copyright © Grove Press Inc., 1972

ISBN 0 352 31092 8

This book is sold subject to the condition that it shall
not, by way of trade or otherwise, be lent,
resold, hired out or otherwise circulated without the
publisher's prior consent in any form of
binding or cover other than that in which it is published
and without a similar condition including this
condition being imposed on the subsequent purchaser.

This book is a work of fiction.
In real life, make sure you practise safe sex.

From the Publishers of
A MAN WITH A MAID:
The Sequel to One of The
Most Famous Erotic Novels
of Victorian England

The Sequel to
A MAN WITH A MAID

Chapter 1

It was about a week after the exciting events in the Snuggery that I had a rendezvous with my beloved Alice and her charming French maid Fanny once again.

During that week I was exceptionally confident, but then I had enough memories to suffice me. And when a virile man like myself finds himself without female solace, there is always the prerogative of finding to one's hand one's male emblem, and while closing one's eyes, dreamily conjuring up those lewd and delicious episodes of past lechery—until suddenly fantasy becomes reality and one feels one's manhood bursting with the pentup sap one has saved since the last encounter with a handmaiden of our goddess Venus.

I must confess that I had half a notion that Lady Bashe and her pretentious daughter Molly might just possibly complain of their treatment in the Snuggery. In our England and in these times of Good Queen Victoria, the female is always the outraged one, and our barristers and justices bow solicitously to their complaints. Now if this plump matron who wished to palm off on me her delightful but rather spoiled and petulant daughter as a mate, had taken it into her vain head to consult a learned solicitor and discover the state of affairs at the Chamber of the Assizes, then I have no doubt that he would have urged her to bring strong action against me. After all, had I not taken her daughter's virginity and compelled them to perform the most intimate acts which one female can perpetrate upon another?

But as the weeks went by, I felt more confident that Lady Betty would not take any such action and that she would try rather to go out of her way never to cross my path lest my presence remind her of the shameful surrender she and Molly had had to make while at the mercy of Connie Blunt, Alice and Fanny.

Connie, alas, had gone to Italy for a fortnight, or I should certainly have called upon her and demanded a private seance, for I needed it now. She had forgotten the rigors of her widowhood and had discovered her own full-blown passionate nature. Connie, that lovely golden-haired girl of about twenty-two years, slight and tall and beautifully formed, with delicious blue eyes and a dazzling skin, had been married only a few weeks when her husband had sustained a heart attack. Whimsically I asked myself whether that heart attack might not have been caused by the initiation of his beautiful blonde wife to the joys of fucking. But then, of course, I recalled that Connie's name was the same as that of her mistress, that she was still a virgin and the marriage had never been consummated. I myself in the Snuggery had discovered this when I probed a delicate forefinger into the delicate pink lips of her snatch and found that she had actually forfeited her maidenhead, though from the tightness of that delicious orifice, one might properly call her an unfucked maiden.

Well, I promised myself that the next time I found Connie Blunt alone, I should ask her to give me the details of her initiation. Perchance she had lost her maidenhead to someone prior to her marriage for that short time. But knowing her voluptuous beauty and how passionately warm-blooded she was, I felt I could ascribe

14

her husband's death to the shattering risk he must have felt when his swollen organ reached for the first time the portals of Connie Blunt's dainty *mons veneris*. And—if he truly had been the one to press through her virgin seal—feel his organ clamped by the tight, moist walls of her exciting channel.

Yes, it would be at least a fortnight before I could confront Connie with my memories of her first fucking, which Alice had so ingeniously arranged. And a week lay ahead of me until Fannie and Alice would return from a trip which the latter had made to visit an elderly aunt in Nottingham.

But I confess the prospect of sublimating my passions in the way that Onan did was not very enticing, not after all these thrilling adventures which I had enjoyed in my newly created Snuggery, and with which doubtless you are familiar, having read the first book of my memoirs. You remember, I am sure, that I began those memoirs by telling you how I had plotted to get Alice into my power after she had cruelly and unjustifiably jilted me. Then, once I had her in my power, after I had literally unveiled the threshholds of her womanly emotions and compelled her to admit to the ardent lust which burned within her tender maiden quim, she became my most passionate ally as well as lover.

I may say at this point that in my thirties I was given the opportunity which few men at my age achieve— that of living like a retired gentleman. My father had been an importer from Australia who had struck it rich in a shop in London. He had befriended a distinguished son of a still more distingushed and influential banker, when the latter found himself set upon by footpads while adventuring one night in Soho and being set upon by thieves while he himself, rash young man, had been in the pursuit of some bordello beauty for whom he lust-ed. Without boring you with such lengthy victories, suffice it to say that the young man's father was so grateful to me for having saved his son from possible injury and certain scandal, that he made known to my father certain advance information concerning debentures and shares and stocks and bonds, which enabled my father to become very comfortably well off. At his death, I, the only heir, received a sizable fortune. Till that time I had been an assistant in a shipping company office for travel and its glamor fascinated me. When I became the sole heir of my father's wealth, I first took a trip around the world and then found myself this apartment in London. I had courted lovely Alice fully expecting to wed her, when the fickle wench jilted me, as you know from the first volume of my memoirs.

But now as I faced a week of inertia, I bethought myself of her married sister, Marion. After the break with Alice which led to so happy an outcome for both of us—even she had said that!—she resorted a little way out of London with a married sister and never seemed to come to town except in her sister's company.

Now I had an interest in this married sister because Alice's lovely maid, whom you may be sure I fucked with as much gusto as I did Alice herself, had confided to me that Marion had only just a few weeks before separated from her husband, having caught him *in flagrante delicto* with a milliner's girl. She had also, Fanny told me, having learned this by listening to her own lovely mistress's gossip, poisoned Alice's mind against me and told Alice that I was no husband for her and still less of a lover.

I gave the darling girl a gold sovereign for that piece of news, which I put away at the back of my mind, intending to pursue it and profit from it when opportunity should provide an occasion. The occasion was now!

I knew that now that I had made Alice mine and also

made of her a conspiratress against Connie Blunt as well as against Lady Bashe and her daughter Molly, that she could not and would not be too vexed with me if I should initiate Marion into those delicious and exciting pleasures which she herself had come to love. More than that, I foresaw that it could be a tableau of absolutely breathtaking and pulse-stirring triumph. If I could actually make Alice apply love potions to her very own sister in the Snuggery.

The more I considered this, the more I wished, helplessly at first, to enjoy Marion all to myself. And that was when I sent a note by messenger to her quarters in Kingsbridge, about three miles to the south of London, asking that she call upon me two days hence at two in the afternoon, as I had information of great importance to her regarding her future happiness now that her marriage had been concluded.

I knew that the curiosity of a woman would be such that, even recognizing my name as one she had damned to Alice many a time, she would not be content until she found out what piece of information it was I had that so concerned her. From chance fancy of mine, as you shall see, a whole new sequence of the most thrilling and lascivious events was destined to take place in the privacy of my little harem, my torture chamber, my bordello deluxe . . . namely, my Snuggery!

Chapter 2

I was not certain that Alice's sister would accept my guileful invitation. Oh, of course I knew that by this time my beautiful mistress must surely have explained to her that all was not well between us. Nevertheless, I could not so easily forgive the brash young woman the annoyance which her wagging tongue had caused me, an annoyance which surely had had a great deal to do with the rift between Alice and myself. I was greatly surprised, therefore, to receive a note back the very next day by messenger informing me that Marion Murdock—that was Alice's sister's married name—would be pleased to call upon me the next day at two in the afternoon as stipulated. She had added a postscript which made me chuckle:

"I must confess I fail somewhat to see what good can be gained by this visit. However, since Alice has told me that she is reconciled with you, I feel I owe it to her future welfare to visit you and decide for myself your true intentions regarding my dear sister, whom I recall you did not treat too well in the past"—and it was signed with her initials, "M.M."

You may recall, if you have read the first volume of my memoirs, that I had originally planned to capture both sisters together and to include Marion in the punishment designed for Alice. Initially that idea had itself not been

unpleasing, because Marion was a fine specimen of female flesh, flesh and blood rather, and a larger and more
stately type than Alice, who was rather petite. One could
indeed do much worse than to have Marion at one's disposal for an hour, to feel and to tickle and to whip and to
fuck!

That stimulus had been so entertaining to my vengeful
mind that I had an armchair made specially at a shop
which did such work, for the project.

The release of a secret catch would set free a mechanism in this chair that would be actuated by the weight
of the occupant, which would instantly cause the arms to
fold and firmly imprison the sitter. The shopowner had
furnished it with luxurious upholstery, and when the
catch was fixed and hidden it surely made the most inviting of chairs. As you will recall, Alice unsuspectingly
chose this chair when she entered the Snuggery ... You
will also recall that on the fateful day of my rendezvous
with Alice which led to the defloration of her maiden
charms and her complete conversion to my will and to
the service of my fucking pleasures, Alice had appeared
alone and had told me that poor Marion had become ill
and had spent such a bad night that she could not come
to town. So in reality you can see, dear reader, I was only
now accomplishing what I had long since planned.

You can imagine with what impatience I sat in my
salon until the bell rang announcing the presence of the
long-awaited married sister, who had caused me such
displeasure and hampered my courting of my beloved
Alice. In order to give her no suspicions, I had refrained
from putting on only my drawers, dressing gown and
slippers; from the first time I had met this paragon of female pulchritude, she had impressed me as being somewhat sanctimonious and prudish as regards such intimate matters as sucking and kissing and cuddling. One

of the things I planned to discover for my very own self this exciting afternoon would be an admission from her own soft lips as to how far she had proceeded with her lately lameted spouse before he had had to shuffle off this mortal coil. So, dressed in my very best, and with my most welcoming smile on my face, I opened the door and greeted Marion.

As I have said, she was a handsome figure of a woman. Alice had been twenty-five at the time of her surrender to me, a true virgin untouched; Marion, unvirgined but for my purposes practically as pure, was two years older. With a swift glance I constated her charms and my heart began to pound. At the same time, too, I must confess to a twitching of my private parts, a trustworthy and never-failing indication that Marion had already begun to rouse the basest carnal desires of which my bachelor nature was capable.

She was about five feet six inches in height, and magnificently proportioned for that stature. Her hair was jet black, whereas Alice's was dark brown; and she wore it in a popular style at the time: a delicious little fringe of affectatious curls all along the top of her high arching forehead, and a prim, huge oval-shaped bun at the back of her head, which suggested somewhat the semblance of a crown. Well, perhaps it was symbolic, for surely she would be my queen of lust for this entire afternoon; and I vowed to myself that I would have her hair unbound and falling in a glossy sheath against her naked skin before she was allowed to dress and return to her own home.

Her nose was a trifle snub, which gave her an aspect of disdain, quite in keeping with what I already knew about her. Her nostrils were widely flaring, quite sensuous, as was her mouth, somewhat small with a pronouncedly ripe upper lip that completed the delineation

21

of insolence and contempt which she appeared so rancorously to show to the male sex. Her eyes were a dark imperious blue, very widely set apart from the bridge of her exquisite nose, and surmounted by exaggeratedly thin-plucked eyebrows and extremely short but thick lashes.

In this period, to be sure, women wore far too many clothes for my immediate savoring pleasure—though contrarily I must admit it was always delightful to prolong the moment of my conquest by having to remove the many garments turn by turn! This paradox heightened my pleasure a good deal, as there was always the element of suspense in wondering just what treasures I should at last espy naked when all the outer conventional costume should be removed and the bare flesh come into ardent view. And from the victim's viewpoint, to be sure, it was far more agonizing, as her suspense was being constantly augmented till the supreme moment of humiliation in finding herself Eve-naked in my presence while I remained fully clothed.

Hence, seeing Marion appear in nominal attire of the fashion would heighten my own excitement, as I could not be too certain as to the embodiment of her delightful curves nor physical charms, save that I had recalled her to have a somewhat slender waist from which—if the bustle's contours could be faithfully believed—there flared impudently rounded, full and ample hips. She did not have so goodly a girth as Lady Betty Bashe, but she nonetheless gave in every way the prospect of being an absolutely breathtaking morsel of pulchritude when she should finally be stripped down to the indisputable state of helpless nakedness that I meant to exact from her as a part of the expiatory punishment she had earned by flouting my courtship of her sister Alice.

There can be no male who finds the opposite sex fascinating and provocative who cannot tremble with hardly suppressed excitement at the anticipation of fulfilling all his most lustful whims. I dare say that in each of us an incipient sadism lingers, product of earlier, less gentle ages when women were slaves and men their lawful masters. Who has not chafed under some haughty girl or woman's scorn, baffled and raging at the knowledge that no retaliatory move is possible under society's code that treats the female as the helpless, weak creature that must be protected at all costs from villainy and violence. And when an inconstant female dares to slap a man solely because he seeks to steal a flattering kiss, he is deemed a blackguard if he even yields to the impulse to raise his hand and give her back measure for measure.

Thus in a sense, man being a rationalizing animal, one might say that in the project of entrapping Marion to atone for her having set my beloved Alice against me, I meant to strike, as it were, a blow for all men who had endured frustration and sarcastic treatment at a woman's hands. And I felt certain that I could dare affronting her without danger from the authorities, precisely because Alice was now fully converted and on my side.

It would have been ideal could Alice have been present on this occasion; I had thought of the fantasy of having her aid me as a lovely, inventive executioner against her very own sister. Then, knowing this to be impossible because of Alice's unavailability in town, I had thought of summoning the eager Fanny, that charming maid who herself was so exquisitely acquiescent in passionate games. But no, this vengeance was rightly mine and no one else's; it must not be shared with any stranger, as Fanny would be to Marion in such a game.

You can therefore imagine with what impatience I awaited the ringing of my bell this fateful afternoon, having envisaged all kinds of the most mouthwatering plans for the consummate and gradual humbling, stripping and fucking of arrogant Marion, who, slightly older than my dear Alice, represented an even more pedestalled and smugly secure kind of female goddess from whose pedestal I meant assuredly to topple her step by infinitely subtle step down to the mire of her degradation and despairing shame!

So all was in readiness at last. I wore presentable attire, not wishing to flout or shock Marion at the very outset—that would come later, when her suspicions had been lulled. It was curiosity that had killed the proverbial cat; it was the same precept which was bringing Marion to my apartment where she would come as respected guest to parlay warily—so she thought!—as to my future intentions towards her sister, only to discover in good time that Alice's fate had already been settled and it therefore impinged upon me only to determine her very fitting own!

And now—the moment had come; the bell pealed at my door, and my heart began to beat more quickly as I went to answer it.

I silently applauded my own impulsive decision to adopt propriety in my clothing, since had I shown myself in dressing gown, Marion would well have believed that "the leopard cannot change his spots" and suspected a trap forthwith. No, in waistcoat and trousers of the finest Ascot cut, even with spats to gild the lily as it were, she could not see me otherwise than as an elegantly attired if worldly gentleman to whom she was coming for a cup of tea and an earnest discussion on her sister's possible betrothal and marriage. Doubtless, I told myself even as I went to the door, she would come full of sententious and pious maxims, ready to sermonize me as to the wrongdoing of my past and her prayerful hopes that my nature would be sanctified in future as regards her only living kin, dear Sister Alice. And to be sure, such a lecture would allow her full occasion for delivering those famous rejoinders full of underlying sarcasm at my expense, while she would bask in the comfortable knowledge that the social code prescribed my accepting them in all meek humility, leaving her safe from reprisal. And then, oh my lady, what a fall from grace there would be!

I opened the door to her. My pulses leaped at the sight that greeted my eager eyes. In an adorable little felt hat with a feather that set a jaunty note of imperious sophistication, cape and rustling silken dress whose hems descended to her ankles, Marion stood before me, her lovely haughty face a bland mask of disdain and smug security; oh, yes, from the very lineaments of her features there could be no doubt she had come to rub salt into my wounds by archly recalling to me that she had never approved of me and that if her sister proved weak enough to succumb to my manly virtues—whose existence she herself still doubted—it was vital that she remain the calm, dispassionate counselor and guide to steer her sister safely through the reefs and treacherous currents which my questionable character was inexorably certain to set before poor helpless Alice as a way of life.

There was a kind of fitting justice to Marion's visit. I had, as my readers will recall, originally had that treacherous armchair in my Snuggery fashioned expressly for the purpose of holding Marion in it and rendering her quite helpless while I went about the delicious procedure of ensnaring her sister Alice and compelling her to submit to my desires. And as you also know, at the last moment, Marion had not been able to keep the appointment—though Alice surely had no reason to complain of lack of attention she had received from me on that occasion!

I kept my face as bland as I could to hide the sudden

delighted emotion that surged through me as I beheld Marion here on the very threshold of my apartment, the first step across which would lead to her coerced surrender and my own sweet revenge! And I congratulated myself upon my wisdom in having agreed to the landlord's insistence that I rent not only my modest suite of sitting-room and two bed-rooms but the unusual "lumber room" —so he had called it—which had once actually been a confinement chamber for lunatics; the house had once been built as a private lunatic asylum, and to this room which I now referred to as my Snuggery, inmates who ultimately were destined for Bedlam had been confined. I may say with some little pride as well as amusement that since my acquisition of this admirably equipped room, it had been put to far better diversions!

Marion wore a fashionable green frock with high collar and full bodice and long, low skirts that were puffed and descended over her ankles. Her fashionable little bonnet tied with laces under her rounded chin, and altogether she was a most prepossessing sort of female. Alice had told me that she had been married three years, and of course I knew that she had been separated from her husband because of his crass infidelity. In my mind, the man must have been a fool to have allowed his wife to discover his penchants for liaisons with other females, since my first glance at Marion made my pulses race and my vital order throb with eager anticipation. There is an old adage that one should be able to eat one's cake and have it too, and assuredly Marion's husband would have done better to have practiced that adage. Never mind, I told myself, I would practice it for him!

"I am here, as you see," she spoke in a cold, disinterested voice, whose inflections showed a rich contralto, whereas Alice had always the most delicious soprano voice—whose timbre never failed to make me shudder with lust when she was undergoing the delightful dalliance with feather or lips or tongue or fingers under my ministrations. Marion's voice pleased me enormously, more than I can say; it suggested such a poise and worldliness as to convince a stranger at first impression that here was a creature who would be in complete control of herself at all times, no matter what the situation. Well, my beauty, I told myself gleefully, this afternoon will see whether or not you are capable of the normal reactions of a trapped and helpless victim! I do not think there's a man alive who has not played with himself the delightful game of conjectural imagery. By which I mean the fanciful visualization of what a fully clothed female must look like when she is bereft of everything except her blushes. As I have already commented, the overly modest and even bulky clothing which was currently fashionable heightened my interest in this little game, and in a sense I had to admit that the more clothing the woman wore, the longer it would take to bring her to this desired state of Eve-nudity. And prolongation is always one of the most exquisite nuances of carnal gratification.

All this flashed through my mind in the space of an instant, needless to say, for I was already replying to Marion's disdainful comment: "And it shall be my pleasant duty, dear Marion, to provide you with a justifiable reason for having made this visit to me. Would you not take a cup with me in my sitting room?"

She swept in, glancing about with her lips pursed in evident contempt of my surroundings, though even Alice had complimented me on their decor and neatness for a bachelor. That was aother black mark against Marion's account which, I, promised myself, I meant to settle to the very fullest measure of my capacities—and hers!— before this afternoon wended its way to its exciting end. Finished with her inspection, she turned back to me and remarked almost insolently, "Mind you, I shan't stay long. The only reason I came, if you must know, was that I had some shopping at the milliner's and at a book store not far from your apartment. And since you made such an important point of communicating with me, I decided to grant you this meeting."

"I'm happy that you did, Marion. Alice has always spoken so favorably of you, and even though you did oppose our knowing each other, I shall hope to persuade you that I am not so black as I have been painted." I did not feel it necessary to add at that point that the painting had been done by Marion herself. Alice had inherently a warm and generous nature—which, to be sure, the sweet pursuit of her conquest had fully unleashed! But I could tell at once that Marion preferred this icy veneer as a kind of shield. Therefore the question was: Was she totally frigid and devoid of warmth and a capacity for passion, or was this veneer only assumed to hide her true outlook? Well, that was precisely the question I had posed myself to have answered for me in my snuggery. I also determined to learn from Marion just how thoroughly her former husband had indoctrinated her into the sweet mysteries of physical bliss. Perhaps he had left me two of her three virginities; the very thought of that nearly made me spill the cup of tea that I was bringing to her and setting beside her with the utmost deference and gentlemanly courtesy. For if you have never had in your apartment an arrogant and cool young woman who treats you as if you were beneath her notice while at the same time you are conjuring up visions of her rosy lips deferentially fixed about your manhood, then you cannot begin to understand the riotous images that filled my mind and the shuddering impulsions which titillated all my nerves and sinews!

After having poured out my own tea and added cream

and sugar to my preference, I seated myself opposite her and fixed upon her the most intent and gracious look it was in my power to muster. An uneasy silence fell over us, and then finally, after a ladylike sip or two from her cup, she set it down in the saucer almost with a clatter as, fixing her dark, widely spaced blue eyes upon me, she remarked, "What chiefly brought me to agreeing to visit you here, Jack, is the inexplicable part of your note to me. I cannot for the life of me understand how you could possess any kind of information about my future happiness, as you termed it, that would be of the least concern to me. Will you please explain your meaning?"

"Now that is a most intimate matter, and I will not be so brash as to give you a direct answer in a single sentence or two, my dear Marion," I told her speciously.

Her supercilious eyebrows arched, and her blue eyes were extremely cold as she retorted, "If you continue the insolence of treating me like a child, Jack, I shall leave at once. I'm already beginning to regret my visit. Now I insist that you be direct with me and explain precisely how you take upon yourself the audacity of telling me that you could possibly know anything about my person or my thoughts or my hopes for the future. You are well aware, I trust, that my husband and I have parted company. You never knew him, and this is the first time thtt you have really met me, and yet out of a clear sky you presume upon yourself to be some sort of judge. This is sheer temerity on your part, and I know now why I was so opposed to my sister's infatuation with you. It appears to me, sir, that you have in you the traits of a scoundrel!"

Mentally I rubbed my hands with glee at this little tirade of hers. How beautifully she had added to her account. She had started a brand-new page and it was already scored most heavily against her. Oh, Marion,

Marion, how little you know me but how well you will before too many hours have passed, I told myself, and I confess that I was hard put to it to keep from smiling like a predatory beast of prey who finds that the elusive gazelle has unwarily entered his lair!

You have made an accusation, Marion," I said as coldly as she had done to me, "that is not seemly, for now you have taken upon yourself the temerity—to use your own picturesque term—of judging me without even knowing me, just as you did before when I first knew Alice. I had never met you when I first knew your lovely sister, and I'm now fully convinced that she jilted me precisely because you had already formed your own opinionated notion of what my character must be. I blamed her at the time, I no longer do so, for we are reconciled. But if your own marriage has come to such a drastic end, Marion, would it not be more reasonable to ask yourself if it is perhaps not you who are at fault and therefore, if that is so, that your opinions and your judgments of people may play you false?"

Color flamed in her cheeks and she imperiously rose. "I knew it was a mistake to come here. I should have known that you would regale me with such an ignoble accusation, sir," she flung at me. "You are a bachelor and an adventurer, and even though Alice tells me that she is most happy in your company, I begin to think that you have had some evil influence upon her. Yes, it must be so. And it is a shocking thing for even a married woman to have to say to a supposed gentleman, that I believe this: I believe that you and my sister have entered upon an illicit liaison which is the more shameful because I had warned her of your selfish and cruel nature, and I am certain that you have no honorable intentions concerning marriage, no matter what favors she may already have granted you."

"I will take you up on that at once, Marion," I told her angrily, for I could not much longer contain my irascibility at these insulting charges. "If indeed there is anything which stands between Alice and myself towards the ultimate happiness of wedlock, it is your own perspicacious determination to set us apart and to make us at odds with each other as you did before. But I have effected this reconciliation and I think that Alice is now wise enough and mature enough in her own emotions as a woman to be no longer influenced by your shrewish whimsies and pronouncements. By what right, I now ask you, do you dare to come into my apartment and to insult me with the epithet of vile seducer and adventurer? What do you know of me except perhaps that which you may have heard by rumour only, since only this day do we first meet face to face?"

At this, Marion tossed her head in high dudgeon and then darting me a look of implacable distaste she haughtily responded: "I see that it is utterly useless, sir, to prolong this discussion further. It is a great mistake for me to have come at all, for I consider you unregenerate and determined to offend me with the tone and tenure of your remarks. I shall ask you, therefore, to show me to the door, and I will take my leave of you. I can only hope that my poor sister comes off better than I begin to believe she will, once having returned to you. But you may be sure that I shall counsel her to the utmost of my abilities to make a complete break with you, sir, and to find herself a gentleman of greater courtesy and proper demeanor when in the presence of the tender sex."

Her formal and, indeed, sanctimonious speech almost made me burst out laughing. She was still a very young woman, for all her marital adventure, and yet she dared to set herself up as a kind of sermonizer, a veritable Mrs. Grundy, who characterized and labeled that which displeased her as necessarily being false and meretricious. Decidedly what Marion needed was being pulled down abruptly and rudely from the preening pedestal on which she had so vauntedly perched herself. And I knew precisely how to bring about that downfall in the Snuggery!

"Why, my dear Marion," I said as blandly as I could, "I deeply regret your hasty conclusion about my motives and my character. I wish you would allow me to demonstrate to you a greater and more reassuring proof that I have only the warmest regard for you just as I have for dear Alice."

You may well conclude, dear reader, that I was not at all mendacious in telling Marion this: for, after all, the attentions which I intended to show her forthwith were as warm as any female, however pretentious or regal of degree, could dream of. And this as quickly as possible! Yes, I was fairly itching to undress the haughty and arrogant older sister of my beloved Alice, to find where the veneer ended and the woman began, where the secret emotions which were bottled up under the elegant gown and the overly modest altogether could be probed and brought to the surface. In a word, dear reader, now more than ever I had determined to make haughty Marion pay dearly for having flouted and insulted me in my own quarters. She had come as a welcome guest, only to pay me back with acid and vinegar for the sweet mead of friendship which I had offered to her.

This little speech of mine did not in the least dissuade her from her intention to leave my apartment without further ado. "You will show me to the door, I trust," she said with a sniff, as she drew herself up to her full stature.

"Of course I will, dear Marion." I smiled as I took her arm and inclined my head in the most humbly deferential of gestures. Even duchesses of the blood royal would have been satisfied with my observance of gallant protocol.

"I did not ask for the support of your arm, sir," she gave me a glacial look as she promptly disengaged her rounded arm, while a look of annoyance made her cheeks flush with anger. "Merely come with me and see that I am properly out of your abode, inside which I never mean to set foot again."

Now, to the right of my sitting room on which the main door to my apartment opens, was the door of the Snuggery. It had doors at each end, and the room was nearly square, of an excellent size and quite lofty. The walls, however, were unbroken, save by the one entrance, as light and air came in from a lantern which occupied the greater part of the roof, and was supported by four strong and stout wooden pillars. The walls were thickly padded, with iron rings let into them at regular distances all around in two rows, one close to the floor and the other about a height of eight feet. From the roof beams dangled rope pulleys in pairs between the pillars; while the two recesses on the entrance side which were caused by the projection of the passage into the room looked as if they had at once time been separated from the rest of the room by bars, as if they were cells at one time. This of course, as I have already indicated and which information I gathered from my landlord at the time when he let my rooms, had come about because the house had initially been used as a private asylum for the mentally unbalanced. It was grim, ironic justice, I thought, that Marion should now make the acquaintance of the Snuggery, because in my estimation she was emotionally unbalanced! I had had the floor covered wtth thick Persian carpets and rugs, and the two alcoves converted into nominal photographic laboratories, but in a

33

way that had made them suitable for lavatories and dressing rooms. As it now appeared—just as it had to dear Alice—it seemed a most pretty and comfortable room where one could chat in quiet and take a glass of port. Of course, it was actually an admirably disguised torture chamber.

I had, in advance of Marion's coming this afternoon, placed a pair of black velvet drapes over the door entering this secret chamber, and I now adroitly led the way towards to that draped entry rather than to my front door. I was able to do this principally because Marion was still reacting from her cholor towards me, and did not notice that instead of taking a straight line to the front door through a little antechamber, she was in reality turning slightly to the right and finding herself against the draped entranceway. I quickly whisked aside the drapes, put my hand to the knob of the door and flung it open, and, with a haughty toss of her head, she passed, not across the little antechamber door, but rather over into that room which was to spell her ultimate downfall and surrender!

Chapter 3

No sooner had Marion crossed the threshold than I closed the door and turned a secret springlock, artfully concealed to one side of a mechanism of the regular knob and lock. I had had this installed shortly after my conquest of dear Alice, and possibly it was a stroke of Providence whch had furnished the inspiration. Perhaps subconsciously I had always dreamed of subjugating and mastering haughty Marion, and this little mechanism would aid me greatly in making the dream now come true!

She glanced around, and then turned to face me, a look of indignation plainly written on her beautiful, insolent features: "Where have you taken me, sir? I told you I wanted to be quits of you, and yet you have led me into another room. Is this part of your trickery and cunning?"

"No, it is part of yours," I said coldly to her, and it amused me to see her recoil and her face turn crimson with anger at this audacious and discourteous retort.

"How dare you!" she drew herself up to her full height, her eyes flashing daggers of enmity at me.

"It appears, Marion, that a man must dare a great deal to overcome your intolerably detestable nature. Even if I had been furnished no details whatsoever, I should be able to conclude for my own analysis of your personality exactly why your husband found it necessary to leave your bed and board," I said with a casual shrug.

She uttered a little cry and then, taking a step forward, slapped me across the cheek. It was a smart, stinging blow, and my eyes widened with delighted surprise. Now she had really added to her account; in fact, she would need an extra page just for that one mark of disfavor in our little ledger. It was already looming into quite a debt.

"Good!" I said, "because now we can be on equal terms. You have insulted me, you have deprecated and disparaged my character without reason or cause, and now you strike me simply because I am candid enough to tell you that it is unfair of you to use your sex as an immunity. If you were a man, Marion, and had dared utter a third of these irritating syllables you have already uttered in my presence, to say nothing of this last courtesy of yours, you would already have merited a sound thrashing with my fists, if not at worst a challenge to a duel. But since you are a woman, and I do not believe and never have believed that a member of the supposedly tender sex should go unrebuked and unscathed for taking unfair advantage of the differences between the sexes, you shall have to be punished in a different way. And I think we shall begin this way."

Saying this, I pushed her into the famous armchair which I have already described, and bent down to touch the mechanism which at once folded its arms around her and clutched her to it as if, inanimate object though it was, it already shared my growing desire for her tasty charms!

"Ohh! What have you done to me? You villian, you brute, you scoundrel! Help!" Marion cried frantically, as she tried to kick her legs and to lift herself out of the chair. But she was pinned as in a vise, and there was no help for her.

"Cry out as much as you like, my dear," I told her coldly, "the room is padded. It was once used to harbor deranged patients, who could evoke a veritable bedlam with their clamoring and yet go unheard outside these walls. If it pleases you to vent your rancor and your thoroughly spiteful nature by shouting, I shall not make any attempt to stop you. In centuries past, they used to bleed patients possessed of a temper; but I find that your cries and your indignation will help to alleviate some of the hot blood that must be surging in your unfriendly self."

Evidently no one had ever talked like that to Marion before, for she regarded me with gaping mouth and dilated eyes, while the heaving of her magnificent bosom told me that she was far from being impervious to my gibes. Also, her struggles had rumpled her skirts and petticoats, so that I was able to catch a glimpse of a very well-turned pair of ankles and the most deliciously sleek calves in all the world, calves which could comparably be displayed side by side with those of her delicious sister Alice and not come off second best.

I contemplated her for a few moments, watching her fume and struggle and send murderous looks in my direction. Indeed, if looks had been able to kill, I should not have been able to accomplish my devious purpose with this very tasty and delectable victim. But instead, I nonchalantly strolled over to two of the pillars, and touching the button set in a panel in the wall, lowered a pair of rope-pulleys so that they would be at the proper height when I moved her under them. For I meant to fasten her by the wrists and hoist her and then leisurely proceed at my own discretion and inclination to ner disrobing. And it would be even more prolonged and discomfitting to her lofty and indomitable nature than the manner in which I had proceeded with sweet Alice.

I nonchalantly lit a cigar and studied her. With her face colored with anger, her large eyes flashing furious thunderbolts which, alas for her, were powerless to deter my will, clutched by the insidious mechanical arms of this ingenious chair, Marion was really a mouthwatering morsel. I could hardly wait to get her undressed and naked, with her legs hugely straddled to bare the most intimate secrets of her anatomy and then to discover whether, for all her lofty airs and impertinent nastiness, she was really possessed of as ardent a temperament as I secretly divined she was. Because I felt certain that all these hostilities displayed in my direction originally stemmed from Marion's own sexual frustration and the disappointment she must have incurred at her husband's infidelity. She was simply trying to take out her own personal deprivations on others usually unfortunate to come in contact with her. But in me, I knew that she had more than met her match!

"Are you feeling more kindly disposed toward me now, and less intent upon doing me bodily harm?" I mockingly asked her as I approached the perfidious chair which clamped her so tightly. I drew in a long savory puff of my cigar, and then breathed it out through my nostrils, till the aromatic heavy smoke reached her and she began to splutter and to choke and cough: "Aaaaah-oh, you wretch, you beast, to treat me like this! I shall go for a constable directly I'm out of this miserable hovel! I shall charge you with assault and bodily harm, sir, and you'll be taken to the Bow Street prison where you belong! Oh, you'll pay for this dearly, sir, and my sister will never again make the tragic error of returning into your clutches!"

38

It took masterful self-control to stand there listening to her tirade while all the time my glittering eyes surveyed her squirming figure and conjecturing what it would be like once the thick outer and inner garments had been removed one by lingering one. I asked myself all sorts of exquisitely salacious questions, such as, would the hair around her cunt be as thick and luxurious and silky as dear Alice's? How would her nipples react to a good tickling with the feather? Would the lips of her cunt moisten and twitch as quickly and as readily as Alice's when the feather was brought to bear against them? What would she do when a man's profaning finger invaded the sacrosanct portals of her body? True, her husband must have had conjugal relations with her, yet in this prudish age in which we lived, my supposition was that he had never attempted anything more than the cohesion between prick and cunt, so therefore Marion must still retain the two entrancing virginities, the dainty little shadowy groove between the cheeks of her voluptuous bottom—would she willingly or unwillingly confess her possession of these treasures?

These and a thousand other stirring queries leaped into my febrile mind at this moment while I enjoyed my cigar and listened to her cries and groans and protests and threats. The more she struggled to be sure, the more she expended her nervous energy and so would become easier prey when the time came to remove her from the chair and to transfer her under the pulleys so that she could be properly fettered, hoisted and stripped.

I had already laid out over an armchair at the other end of the room, a silk dressing gown and slippers. Once I had tied Marion, I should let her wait my pleasure while I calmly proceeded to make myself thoroughly comfortable and at my ease. The thought of having her at my mercy while my naked flesh was covered only by the delightfully soft, titillating silk robe was already an enormous delight to anticipate. Yes, I have often felt pity for the man who, while undoubtedly possessed of as much virility and passion as I myself contain, but lacks the ingenuity and inventive knowledge to draw out his pleasures, to taste every possible subtle nuance of mental and visual stimulus, which is the only sensible way to enjoy the pleasures of Cythera which our goddess Venus has vouchsafed to mankind apt and astute enough to profit from her generosity.

Finally, when I had almost finished my cigar, I asked her, "If I release you from the chair, will you apologize for striking me and for all these insults?"

Her bosom heaving, in a hoarse, shaking voice, she immediately responded, "Never! I would rather die than apologize to a scoundrel like you! Oh, you have not heard the last of this, sir! You coward, to take advantage of me and to trap me, to hold me here against my will, to bruise me with this diabolical chair which is crushing me abominably! I shall bring civil suit against you, once you have spent a suitable time in prison for your nefarious conduct this afternoon!"

I asked myself whether Marion used this highflown verbiage when she had been in bed with her former husband. Decidedly if she had, I could see one reason the more why he had left her for another woman who talked less and acted more honestly. I even asked myself whether she had ever yielded herself to him completely naked, as Alice had learned to do with me. Or whether, yielding at all, she had achieved pleasure for herself and would be honest enough to admit it. Well, all these questions and many more which would arise at the moment and by and from the moment, would be answered by the delicious Marion before she would be allowed to set foot outside the Snuggery. That was my resolve, and the pursuit of my resolve is what I shall now narrate.

Chapter 4

I took a last look around the Snuggery, to remind myself once again of all its delightful propensities for subjugating a naughty, rebellious young woman like Marion. Not far from the pillars was an immense divan-couch upholstered in dark leather, standing on eight massive legs (four on each side), behind each of which lay, coiled for use, a strong leather strap which was worked by rollers hidden in the upholstery. Cushions were piled all over it to dissemble its actual role, that of a coercional whipping bench or couch of amorous surrender. Yes, everything was in place, and now the moment had come to transfer Marion from her immobilized pose in the armchair to a standing position from which I could leisurely proceed to caress and undress her to my heart's content . . . a euphemistic expression if ever there was one, for actually it would be to my prick's content!

I took a last puff of my cigar and crushed it out in a copper ashtray on a little tabouret next to the armchair in which the fuming beauty was incarcerated. She gave me a furious look of hatred, glancing at the cigar, which I had purposely not put out, so fumes of smoke still rose towards her.

"So you are still of a mind not to apologize, Marion!" I resumed my preliminary interrogation.

She did not deign to reply, but instead turned her face

away and drew a long, shuddering breath. It was obvious that she was trying to impress me with the attitude that she could not bear the sight of me. Ah, but I would-*bare* the sight of her, and then poor Marion would just have to grin and bear it!

"Oh, well," I said calmly, "I shall let you go."

"And high time, too!" she angrily retorted. "But don't think, sir, that you can attempt to soothe my feelings by releasing me. I am still determined to prefer charges against you for your rude and ungentlemanly assault upon my person. You had absolutely no right to hold me here against my will, sir. It is a criminal thing, as you will soon find out!"

"That we shall see, my dear Marion," I replied as I touched the secret mechanism of the chair. The arms folded back and Marion was able, with a smothered cry of frustrated anger, to put her arms on the edges and to lift herself to her feet. Hardly had she done so, however, when I pounced upon her, grasping her by the shoulders and forcing her over to the dangling rope pulleys.

Now, these rope pulleys had already been admirably tested on her sister, as you will recall, and I had then used an endless band of the softest, strongest silk rope I could get made. The ropes and straps in the Snuggery were all fitted with swivelsnap hooks. All I had to do was slip a double band around Marion's waist or ankle, pass one end through the other, draw it tight, and then snap the free end into the swivel hook. No matter how much she should struggle or twist or plunge about, she could not loosen this attachment, a fact I had already learned when I conquered Alice. Moreover, the softness of the silk would prevent her finely grained skin from being rubbed or even marked, yet at the same time I could proceed with the utmost ruthlessness. Marion had been taken by surprise, as I had hoped she would be. She was practically under the rope-pulleys by the time she recognized my purpose, and she began to utter wild cries, and to struggle and to strike at me with her fists. I disregarded her buffets entirely, concentrating on seizing her wrists with both hands; then, grasping the nearest rope-pulley, I fastened it securely around her wrists. This done, it was a matter of another moment or two to attach her other wrist the same way. I then touched the button, the ropes tightened inexorably, Marion's arms were drawn upwards until they were stretched to the maximum, and she was forced to stand erect from the pull exerted on her slender wrists.

"You villain! Untie me at once! How dare you treat me this way, you abominable man? What are you going to do to me? I warn you, you will suffer for this brutality!" Marion cried in a vibrant, shaking voice as she began to kick, while at the same time dragging on her bound wrists.

I watched carefully, and when I was certain that the admirable device of the silk bands attached to the swivel hooks would surely hold and that she absolutely could not free herself, I calmly went to the other armchair at the other end of the room, where my dressing gown and slippers awaited me. I had put up a Japanese shoji screen beside the armchair, and I retired behind it now, leaving Marion to cry out and inveigh against me while I simply undressed completely, then donned the dressing gown and belted it tightly, thrust my bare feet into slippers, and emerged from behind the screen.

When she saw me approach her in such intimate attire, her large eyes enormously dilated and her mouth gaped with the most consternated surprise I have ever seen on a woman's face. All she could say was "Ohhh!"

It was certainly a good beginning. I had managed at

45

last to divert her arrogant and selfish nature from the righteous indignation which was consuming her.

Now, perhaps for the first time, she realized that she had been most rash in flouting me and behaving in no way as a well-bred feminine guest should ever do in a gentleman's apartment.

Decidedly, she was quite feminine. The charming little fringe of exaggerated curls all along the top of her forehead contrasted with the prim bun into which her black hair was gathered at the back of her haughty head. Her dark blue eyes were glistening with undisguised rage, and I could not help but mark the angry curl of her ripe upper lip. Her complexion was quite good, and it foretold the most indescribably delicious moments for me when I should at last have every inch of it exposed to my eager gaze. Alice had ivory skin, but Marion's skin in some ways excited me now even more: it was a warm olive in tone, and that is a complexion which I had always believed to denote an ardent temperament.

"Are you quite through staring, you contemptible brute?" she suddenly ranted, and before I could anticipate her conduct, kicked out her right foot at me. It was by great good luck only that I managed to recoil, or she might have kicked me very painfully in the shin or knee-cap.

"I have hardly begun, Marion," I answered, "but it seems to me that you are trying to impede my view." It was evident to me, however, that, unlike Alice, who finally realized the futility of struggling against the inevitable, Marion was made of sterner stuff and would continue to rebel against my intentions and therefore hamper my full enjoyment of her luscious charms. "I shall have to take measures to quiet your angry spirit, "I said jestingly.

Now there were rings set at the base of the pillars as

well as at a point about eight feet from the floor. These lower rings would be extremely handy, for as I moved to one side of Marion, she launched another perfidious kick at my person, indicating that she did not intend to submit quite so readily as might be hoped.

So I procured two long silken ropes, after having measured the distance between the pillars and where she stood, and I moved to her right, squatted down, seized her left ankle with my left hand and wound the silken rope around her slim ankle with several turns, making a good strong knot. Next I secured the other end through the ring at the base of the pillar, which immobilized that leg. It did not take long to treat the other leg the same way, and by then, I assure you, Marion was in a perfect frenzy of hateful rage. To her credit, I must say that she had as yet displayed no fear, and I must say also that the sight of her sparkling eyes, her furiously flushed face, her defiant wriggling against her bonds, and the hoarse and insulting threats which she poured forth against me as I proceeded to immobilize her for the preliminary conquest of her person whetted my sexual appetites to a boundless flight of rapture.

"That's better, Marion. Now we shall be able to conduct a rational conversation, without your being able to interrupt it with unladylike kicks," I said as I approached her.

"You utter swine," she hissed between her teeth, "you are showing yourself in your true colours at last. Oh, I knew from the start, I knew intuitively what a dreadful mistake my poor sister made in ever becoming attached to you. But you wait, you dreadful monster, till I get out of here, and you will not be able to assault and maltreat any more helpless girls, I promise you."

"And I, for my part, Marion," I told her deliberately, staring into her eyes with a mocking expression on my face, "promise you that you shall not leave here till you have given me even more than your lovely and gentle sister has done, and that many times over."

She read my meaning all too well. She seemed to recoil in her bonds, as if throwing herself backwards away from me. Her eyes widened enormously, and then a sudden, fiery color suffused her olive-sheened cheeks.

"Since you have had the advantage of marital experience and estate over dear Alice," I resumed in my most taunting tones, "I expected that you would be more perceptive and would require less explanation of my feelings for you, Marion. You have an admirable figure, and it is plain to see why you attracted your husband. What I intend to find out, however, is why you failed to hold him, always assuming that he was as virile and appreciative a man as I myself. Yes, quite an excellent figure, although I personally should not choose so thick a fabric for your dress. It only hides the elegance of your bosom."

"How dare you!" she managed in a shuddering, low, husky voice

"I shall dare a great deal before you leave here, Marion. And before you do, you will have paid me back for every slander, every slur, every haughty and insolent look, every threat and curse and vilification. And then there is that infamous slap you rendered me, thinking yourself beyond reprisal simply because of your sex. It is going to be a long afternoon for you, I fear. Let me see now, how shall we begin? But of course—I must see if those splendid breasts are as firm as they seem to be through your bodice!"

"What do you mean? You infernal fiend—I forbid you to touch me! If you do—I will kill you, I swear I will, as soon as I am free," she cried in an almost hysterical frenzy.

Looking up at the ceiling, she dragged ferociously on

her wrists, but she did not succeed in loosening them to the slightest degree. And, much to my delight, her violent maneuvers made her breasts jiggle in the most suggestive way. I watched her greedily, waiting for her to come to the awareness that, despite all her bravado and defiance, she was doomed.

But from the savage rancor on her lovely, arrogant face, the fulminating surge of her magnificent bosom, and the convulsive jerks she continued to give to her pinioned wrists, it was evident that she was still a long way from that realization. As for myself, my cock was swelling and aching with the infinitesimal relish of the mysterious delights I meant to provide for it before this long and delicious afternoon had been concluded.

"Can it be, my dear Marion," I pursued a new track now, "that all this hostility of yours originates from your jealousy of Alice?"

She was startled by this unexpected question, for she looked at me with a piercing, questioning gaze, and her fine forehead furrowed as she strove to catch my meaning. Before she could reply, I continued in the same bantering tone, "Perhaps with you it is a case of sour grapes, my charming sister-in-law to be."

"You contemptible liar!" was her angry, hoarse retort. "You have no more intention of marrying Alice than does the man in the moon, and you will not have the chance, for I intend to inform her once and for all of your heinous character, you odious blackguard!"

"It has been said by many a famous writer, my dear Marion," I ignored her furious insult, "that hate is akin to love. Well, presuming that is so, you must secretly love me very dearly to hate me so, or at least to profess that you do."

"I—love you! Oh, you are impossible! I will not say another word to you except to warn you that if you do not release me at once, you will repent it till your dying day!" was her panting reply.

I drew up a chair and seated myself before her. She caught her breath and bit her lower lip, staring down at me. Now, perhaps for the first time, I could detect a hint of fear in those dark blue, imperiously cold eyes, for they now held a shadow of uncertainty. Almost instantly, however, she looked upwards and jerked strongly at her wrists, finding it difficult to balance herself, for the ropes at her ankles had drawn her legs slightly apart—though not to their fullest extent—and the traction in two directions was proving to be a sore trial for her.

"I assure you they will hold you fast till I deign to let you down, Marion. Yes, you are quite attractive, and I think you know it. I think perhaps you give yourself too many fine airs, and this may be one reason why you are no longer united with your husband. But quite beyond that, and let us be honest at this moment if at no other," I blandly continued, "is it not the truth that having learned that I am really not such an odious person after all and that my prospects and my person are quite sanguine, you resolved that if you could not have me you would make certain Alice would not either? This, my dear Marion, is the very quintessence of sour grapes."

"You are absolutely insane, sir, to even suggest such a despicable thing," and her voice trembled as her magnificent bosom began to heave wildly again. "I detest and abominate you, do you understand? If it meant my very life, I would never submit myself to you, and the thought that you have been able to enjoy my sister as intimately as I know you have—for her stupidly radiant behaviour has told me that without her having had to say a word about what has passed between the two of you—really makes me quite ill!"

"But if Alice has not told you—to use your words, my

50

dear Marion—what has passed between us two, you have no realistic basis for your repugnance. I mean to put you in a practical way of understanding just what does occur between a man and a woman. It may well be a lesson that you stand in need of, considering that you could not hold your husband for all your delightful charms. And now, with or without your leave, I am going to learn for myself something of their nature."

I had seated myself in this chair, just as I had done with her sister, only with Alice I had not bothered to bind her ankles because she had not thought of kicking me. I now placed my hands on Marion's waist, and she at once uttered an angry cry and twisted herself back from me.

"I warn you, sir, I warn you," she panted. "If you do me any indignity, you will expiate your crime in prison and for as long a time as I can have my solicitor charge you!"

"Well, since you have already determined to have me languish in a cell, my dear sister-in-law to be," I retorted merrily, "I may as well be hanged for a wolf as a sheep." So saying, I slipped my hands behind her shapely back and moved them round until they were at the sides of her breasts.

Marion uttered a wild cry and twisted and dragged at her wrists, to no avail. Gnashing her teeth, her eyes bulging with fury and now a definite fear, she tried to evade my unwanted caresses. I prolonged the moment to the longest possible degree, and then I boldly cupped the globes of her bosom through her clothes!

"Ohh! I forbid you—you inhuman monster. Stop that at once, you vile, lecherous fiend—Oh, help, for God's sake, help me! I am at the mercy of a monster," she shrieked.

I dropped my hands at once, letting her think she had

won her point, for when I next pursued my devious designs upon her, it would be the more shattering to her enervated psyche. I stared up at her, seeing how violently her face was flushed, her lips trembling, her eyes exorbitant, her forehead deeply furrowed, and, delicious telltale sign, a bead or two of sweat appearing along her high forehead at the fringe of those flouncy, affectatious curls.

Her breath was erratic, and her nostrils flared and shrank as she tried once again to wrest herself free.

Now, Alice's breasts were firm, upstanding, saucy, and inviting. Perhaps a trifle too full for perfection, but they were also set rather widely apart, and the aureolae were wide and of a most delicious soft pink hue, in whose centers nuzzled dainty little crinkly buds. Yet from the first tentative palpation I had had of Marion's bosom, it had seemed to me that her breasts were rather closely set together and splendidly shaped like firm ripe pears with an uptilting verve to their crests. Even through the thickness of dress and bodice and perhaps the camisole which she must be wearing, her flesh seemed to me to be wonderfully resilient and jouncy. It was a magnificent augury of what was to come.

In the pocket of my dressing gown I had deposed a pair of shears. These I had used to dispossess Alice from the confinements of her final veils. There can be no doubt that once a woman is stripped naked, and no matter how obdurate or insolent her nature, she cannot but sense an atrocious loss of pride and dignity when in the presence of her disrober. Well, I was counting on that in my final plans for the final subjugation of arrogant and beautiful Marion.

I should say that she was about an inch taller than Alice, though the rather bulky way she was dressed suggested an even greater plumpness than her sister had in fact. This is why the disrobing of a charming woman is such a treat for a connoisseur of feminine pulchritude: until the very last moment he is kept in suspense as to the true beauties of the body he is about to lay bare for his carnal appeasement.

When I saw that the heaving of her bosom had somewhat subsided, I took hold of her waist again with both my hands and caressed it. Marion shuddered and closed her eyes, setting her teeth to keep from uttering a word. It was evident that she wished to give her executioner not one ounce of satisfaction. It was equally evident that she wished to give the impression of death before dishonor, which was rather ludicrous, after all, in a married woman. But it was totally in keeping with her affectatious and holier-than-thou personality. *Yes, Marion, we are going to strip away that veneer of yours along with your clothes,* I told myself.

Again and completely at my leisure, I considered her. She was damnably delicious, now that there was proof of her being somewhat less than an icy, untouchable goddess, a statue posed high above me on a pedestal. Now the gleam of sweat was more evident than before on her forehead, and long, shivering tremors swept along her tractioned arms and shoulders, while her face was flushed and taut with a mounting anxiety that insidiously began to gnaw against all her angry and heroic defiance. She realized that she was well caught and vulnerable, but I do not think she believed, even at this moment, that I would really go so far as I planned to do; undoubtedly the prim propriety of her upbringing and her outlook on marriage—though here, I will confess, I was speculating—made it absolutely inconceivable that a man should take and pinion and strip and feel and then have his way with her.

"If you were not quite so rebellious, my dear Marion,"

I now coolly remarked, "the two of us could be far more comfortable than I fear you are at this moment. However, Goethe has an admirable proverb which I shall render for you in the English translation. 'What you can do without, do without.' I fear, therefore, that I must content myself with the sparse means at my disposal till you show a less unruly nature."

And with this, rising from my chair, I pressed myself against her till our knees met and my hands moved round to press against her shoulders so her bosom could not evade my eager chest. Thus her face was posed inches from mine, and I could hear the rapid, agonized stress of her breathing as well as see the broadening of her lovely nostril-wings and read also in her dilated eyes the glazed shadows of her rising dread. She jerked convulsively against my hands, but I nonetheless thrilled to feel her fine, firm breasts mashing against my chest, outlining their rondures against the thick cloth which kept their olive-satiny goblets from my entranced gaze and touch. She twisted her face to the left, closing her eyes as another long shiver ran through her. Now I could see the fine beads of sweat all along her forehead and at the sides near those dainty ears, indisputable proof of her terrifying uncertainty, of the loss of her vaunted poise and arrogance . . . the first true triumph against this embattled, beautiful young virago!

I could savor each triumph in its turn and time, and I was not greedy, though I confess it required the most powerful self-control of which I was capable to keep from altering my schedule of devestiture of Marion's raiment and the progression to tactual and erotic torments and tauntings which would finally wreak havoc on her delicious, naked, helpless person.

The cords of her round throat surged against the warm olive skin, and I saw the triphammering of the lovely little pulse at the soft hollow which told of her overwrought excitement and increasing anxiety. She had compressed her lips and kept her eyes tightly closed, trying to obliterate me in the manner of the ostrich which thrusts its head into the sand to deny the existence of the oncoming hunter. The time had therefore come to show her that I could not simply be wished away and that my will was stronger than hers, to say nothing of my desire.

So, stealthily releasing her quivering shoulders, I placed my palms at her waist, just at the curve of her rounded hips, which seemed much fuller than they probably were because of the width and fullness of the skirt, and then, without warning, I clapped my palms solidly against the cheeks of her bottom!

"Aahhh! You filthy devil—oh, my God, take your dirty hands away at once, you unspeakable, detestable, horrible beast!" was Marion's almost hysterical outburst. She lunged from side to side, throwing back her head towards the ceiling, but all she could see was the ceiling and the inexorable pulleys fixed in that firmament, and there was no reprieve in either. I pressed my palms more firmly against her behind, and with a groan, Marion pressed herself more closely against me, meanwhile glancing back and down at herself as if hoping that this was a nightmare and what she was experiencing was only a figment of her feverishly exercised imagination.

To rid her of that absurd notion, I spread my fingers fantail against the plump globes of her bewitching backside, and then I squeezed!

"Ohh! You beast—no, I don't want you to touch me! You infamous scoundrel, you blackguard—take your hands away from me at once!" she stormed. Her voice trembled and shook with agonized and powerless rage as she trembled and shook with anger. Even as I stared at her contorted face, I could see the deepening of her blushes; and the effect of crimson against that olive skin, was, I must tell you, devastatingly exciting for me. My cock was now impatiently demanding some kind of participation in the fray, for I felt it swell and throb violently, lifting out the folds of my dressing gown until, had Alice's sister chanced to lower her eyes and peer down between our bodies, she could not have mistaken the nature of my own excitement.

"From the frantic wrigglings my touch seems to produce in you, Marion," I remarked as I momentarily relaxed the grip of my sinewy fingers, "I am beginning to believe that your nuptials must have been thoroughly intellectual rather than carnal. What? Do you intend to imply to me that your husband did not hold you this way when he took his conjugal rights?"

"Ohhh!" Her gasp was utterly scandalized. She turned her face to the other side now, but her eyelids blinked rapidly and I thought I saw the suspicion of glistening tears in their shadowed depths. Her fingers clawed the air, and once again she wrenched feverishly at her bound wrists.

"Yes," I continued banteringly, "one would think you a virgin, Marion, from the way you squirm and gasp at the slightest liberty one takes with your delightful person. But surely the marriage must have been consummated in the time of three years."

"Oh, you—you demon—you horrid, overbearing, boorish swine!" she panted, and she turned on me such a withering look of feverish hatred that I almost quailed.

"As I remarked a little earlier," I at last countered her insult, "in the olden days physicians used their lancets to bleed a patient whose humor was choleric, lest he have apoplexy or be stricken with an attack of overly tautened nerves. You are overly hot, and I think the reason is the excessive clothing you are wearing. It is true the room is

56

somewhat close. So instead of bloodletting, Marion, I shall put you somewhat more at your ease by removing some of your apparel."

"Oh God, no! You have no right! I forbid you—this is criminal, horrible, vile. Oh, help! Help, in the name of mercy! Will no one help me from this monster?" she shouted. Again she twisted to and fro and dragged at her ropes.

I put my left arm around her waist and with my right hand began to stroke her hip and bottom, totally ignoring her cries and gasps and groans, and managing her desperate wrigglings with the grip of my circling arm. Again her head fell back, but this time her eyes were closed and only the trembling of her lips and the convulsive flickering of her nostrils told me what she was experiencing. So, too, did the tumultuous surging of her bosom which strained at the stuff of her dress as if longing to be liberated from its prison.

"Patience, Marion," I told her mockingly. Now seating myself on the chair again and keeping my left arm around her waist, I verified the appraisal I had already made of her hips and bottom by pressing my right hand even more firmly and tightly against those delicious curves. From what I could determine, she was about to show me a figure at least as enticing as sweet Alice's. How could a husband have left such a treasure without having educated her into all the ways of bliss that can be procured between a man and a maid? It must only be because she was not willing, or too prudish, or finally, because her husband was an utter fool. I would not make the same mistake he had made, I told myself.

At last I finished with the examination of her bottom, all throughout which she had groaned and squirmed and jerked uselessly at her wrists. She also made desperate attempts to close her widened thighs, quite unaware

57

what a suggestive pose she was proffering even against her will, but of course the ropes at her ankles refused to yield even so much as an inch.

I released her waist also, and for a long moment I stared up at her, gloating at her confusion and feverish anxiety. She was biting her lower lip repeatedly now, and I could see that the beads of sweat had fallen from her forehead, down her cheeks almost like tears. Her thick, long lashes fluttered almost incessantly. Decidedly, Marion's nerves were at a state of flux and she was at that impressionable stage when she could no longer be mistress of herself so long as there was a master like myself present to direct her course.

Chapter 5

Once again I rose from my chair and, pressing myself tightly against the fuming young woman, cupped my hands around her voluptuous, firm behind and pressed her tightly up against me. She uttered a raging cry and struggled vainly to break loose, tilting back her head until the cords of her neck stood out against the soft, warm olive skin in the most obvious display of aversion to my person. Her lips curled back to bare fine, strong, white teeth, and altogether she presented the most alluring portrait of rebellious femininity at bay that I had ever encountered. I was greatly pleased with Marion; by contrast, sweet Alice had succumbed with far less hostility. But this duel which I foresaw between Marion and myself could only procure me a thousand more new and seductive joys which would redound to the more crushing defeat of Marion herself!

By this time, also, she could have no doubt of the state of my own emotions as I kept her pressed tightly against me. My angrily stiff prick at last demanded its rightful emergence into the sphere of action, so to speak, and thrust out boldly through the folds of my dressing gown. The broad meatus, that valiant spearhead on which I proposed to skewer haughty Marion's proud citadel, rubbed against the hollow of her dress where I knew her crotch to be. And the burning waves of furious, crimson-

59

ing shame which beleagured her now told me that she was quite sensible as to my intent, as well as to the adequacy with which I had come prepared to wreak my male vengeance for her effrontery.

My hands now left her bottom to rove down the backs of her thighs, pressing her full skirts tightly up against them so I could shape out those luscious columns. I felt them quivering and jerking against my appraising palpations, and stiffled gasps emerged from between her clenched teeth, while her lashes fluttered and her eyelids blinked repeatedly as she stubbornly twisted her face as far from me as she could get it. But her body, rather more than her face, deliciously told me that she was not quite so impervious to my ministrations as she would have it appear, and as I pressed the head of my cock directly against her veiled grotto, I knew that the moment had come at last to carry out my decision of disrobing her, step by mortifying step.

Without a word of warning, therefore, I released her thighs, at which she gave a gasp, no doubt of relief, only to commence with the dainty mother-of-pearl buttons down the middle of her handsome chest. One by one I began to open these, while she stared at me for a long moment as if unwilling to believe that I would go so far as this. But when I had reached the final button, she said in a shuddering, hoarse voice: "You villain, what are you going to do to me now? I warn you, treating a decent woman like this will mean prison for life for an unprincipled wretch like you!"

"Why, my dear Marion, since it is already certain that you mean to send me to prison for merely tying your wrists above your head just to give you pause for meditation," I tauntingly replied, "I may as well have some little pleasure for my trouble, to provide some pleasant memories for the period of my incarceration in a cell. Don't you think so?"

I now unfastened the two tiny buttons of the high collar of her frock, and this gave me full leeway to take hold of the yawning flaps from her throat down to the lower curves of her bosom and energetically rip the frock asunder at the front, exposing a short pink crinoline blouse under which was evidently a tight, white linen bodice. I smiled with amusement at this discovery, for it showed me that Marion was not only fastidious but also extremely prudish in keeping herself so voluminously veiled. For once, therefore, I did not regret this abundance of garments; the removal of each in turn would augment her anxiety and shame and frustrated rage, and thus heighten my own exquisite and gloating pleasures in this conquest of Alice's over-righteous sister.

"I shall, of course, replace this ruined frock, Marion," I remarked as I proceeded to unfasten the blouse. She uttered a cry of horror and resumed her struggles to get free. She lunged backwards and then to the side, energetically tugging at the tethered wrists, but her face was congested and red with the violent waves of crimson sweeping over her, both from her exertion and her mortification. The visions I had of the skin of her warm upper chest and throat were enough to enflame my determination to husk her completely naked. There was on her collarbone to the left a most adorable little brown, oval-shaped birthmark, which I playfully stroked with a fingertip while I paused to let her take stock of her situation. In this dishevelled disarray, standing with legs slghtly spread and arms tractioned above her head, her face scarlet and her teeth chattering, her sensuous nostril-wings flaring and shrinking, and her large eyes blinking uncontrollably as, no doubt, she fought away the treacherous tears of anguish which all this was causing her, Marion at this moment excited me even more than had my beautiful Alice at the moment of the latter's subjugation. I was not ashamed of myself for this fickle transfer of affections; a prick has no conscience and it is entirely a creature of hedonism, no matter how cerebrally its owner may be motivated. Had Alice been in Marion's place at this moment, my prick would doubtless have had as great an exuberance, but Marion must now bear the brunt of its desires.

Now at last I reached the bodice, and I extended my right hand toward the dainty buttons, while my left moved behind her to palm the small of her back so that she might not lunge away from me. As my fingers touched the first button, she panted in a choking voice: "In God's name, no—don't do this to me, sir—if—if you mean to frighten me, then be sure you have. I am dying of shame—I—I entreat you to be merciful!"

"But I am being merciful, Marion; for all your jibes and slander, as well as for your slap, I might, had I been more ruthlessly inclined, have taken a whip to those soft shoulders and that plump backside whose dimensions I am longing to behold, after having felt you just now. No, quite the contrary, Marion. You see in me an admiring spectator standing ready to salute your hidden charms, and you cannot accuse me of cruelty. It is rather you who are guilty of that for hiding your delicious person with such a confining amount of garments."

"Ohh, you—you wicked, heartless, infamous man!" she breathed, turning her face to the left, closing her eyes and compressing her lips, while a long shudder rippled through her body.

I now unbuttoned her bodice, and as the last button gave way to my impetuous fingers, she uttered a low groan and bent her head a little, trembling convulsively as she felt me drag apart the folds and expose in all their glory the sumptuous turrets of her naked bossom.

I almost gasped myself in ecstatic admiration. Marion's breasts were really splendid, boldly uptilting pears with the sauciest, firm dark coral nipples imaginable. The aureolae were wide and of a brownish-orangeish hue, and I could not take my eyes off them for a long, devouring moment. But when at last I extended my hands and cupped those firm, satiny-warm gourds, my thumbpads delicately pressing the pert buds back into their centers, Marion uttered a shriek of shame and rage, and violently flung herself backwards to escape the ignominious palpation.

How I reveled in the warm, palpitating feel of her naked breasts against my eager hands! Her panting, sobbing and tumultuous breathing made them flutter like doves in my avid grasp, while she turned her face from side to side, her forehead now damp with agony-sweat, continuing to jerk at her bound wrists and claw the air uselessly with her long, slim fingers. I knew that she longed to rip and shred my face with her sharpbuffed nails if she were free, and the knowledge that she was utterly at my mercy and must endure all that I cared to inflict upon her, filled me with a glorious exuberance and an incomparable vitality. My prick ached so savagely that I determined to give her a brief respite so that she could once more reappraise her situation, which was certainly no more desperate than at the outset.

I seated myself before her while I planned the next step in my campaign to subjugate haughty Marion. You will recall that I had had to undress Alice forcibly, though I had not needed to use the scissors; I very much doubted, however, that Marion would give me tne same kind of passive resignation, allowing me to work her clothes over her clenched hands, over the ropes, then release each rope in turn, slip the garments down and off, then refasten the noose. No, it would actually be more exciting to cut away Marion's clothes when the moment came to expose the most intimate parts of her body. I had already ripped her frock down to the waist, badly enough so that it would certainly need replacement. I therefore lit a fresh cigar and sat there silently watching her while I puffed away, sending puffs of smoke into her scarlet, contorted face. She coughed, twisted her face from side to side, clenched her teeth and moaned, trying her best not took at me during this prolonged interlude. All this while I feasted my eyes on the shuddering rise and fall of those heaving loveglobes, whose nipples seemed to have darkened and stiffened now that they were exposed to the air and to the burning caresses of my enraptured gaze.

"Well, Marion, are you beginning to realize that your sharp tongue and impulsive belligerence have condemned you to reprisal?" I mockingly asked after this long silence.

"Have—have you no decency in your nature, s-sir?" she at last forced herself to speak, and her voice was low and husky and trembling with the effort it must have cost her. "Very well. I admit that I behaved rudely to you, and I should not have slapped you, but that gave you no right to abuse me and to shame me in this way, which is criminal, as you surely know. Let me go now, at least, to make some amends for your disgraceful and horrid conduct. In return, I—I will apologize for having slapped you."

"What, so soon contrite, after so determined and embittered a resolve to have me imprisoned, Marion?" I chuckled, as I took a long puff at my cigar and sent a wreath of aromatic blue smoke into her contorted face. "I confess I like you better as an enraged Amazon, ready to claw and rend and decimate me at all costs. So you are willing to apologize for the slap, are you? And do you think, Marion, that will even the score between us, Marion? You, who from the outset tried in every way to hamper my romance with your sister. You, who constantly blackened my character, even before we had come to that first rift which was your doing, trying to set her mind against me and to deny her her own natural inclinations."

"You are a heartless wretch to have so entrapped me," she panted, frantically glancing down at her front and biting her lips again as she saw how lewdly the ripped front of her frock, the yawning blouse and bodice, exposed the glories of her olive-sheened, panting naked bosom "You dared lure me here by saying that you could inform me of my future happiness, only to brutalize and manhandle me in this abusive and criminal way—surely whatever I have done to you is more than wiped out by the offense you have given me this afternoon."

"Not by one thousandth part, I fear," was my reply as I leaned back in my chair and leered up at her, giving her a taste of her own medicine, as it were. "You very nearly cost me my sweetheart, you dared to set yourself up as judge and jury over me, whereas now I merely pay an admiring tribute to your womanly attributes, Marion. Indeed, I have been asking myself all this time if you were truly a woman, to have so little heart and so much spleen and so much vindictiveness."

"And that is a damnable lie!" she burst out, her naked bosom heaving wildly as she struggled with the bonds that held her. "I could not possibly in all the world have the slightest regard for a beast and traducer like you, even if you were the only man alive!"

"Now that is much better, and I much prefer it. It comes from the heart and is therefore more credible," I mockingly told her. "And I did not lie when I told you I would give you information as to your future happiness. I shall proceed to do that, Marion, by continuing with my plan to draw from you even more truthful and sincere reactions which will once and for all set to rest in my mind the doubts I have had. For all this while you have represented yourself as a stone statue, with no more heart than that and no more soul and no more understanding of what may pass between a man and a maid who desires him. Prepare yourself, then, to learn the absolute truth about yourself before this afternoon is ended."

I crushed out my cigar in the ashtray and rose from my chair. Marion sucked in her breath, her eyes widening supremely, and tried to fling herself backward at my approach. Once again I put my hands out to those splendid naked globes of her bosom and lovingly squeezed and stroked them, feeling her nipples stiffen and tingle as my palms lingeringly grazed those crinkly tidbits. Then once again I seated myself and, while I kept my eyes on her scarlet and contorted face, I lowered my hands under her voluminous skirts and suddenly yanked them up.

"Oh my God, no! Don't do that! Oh, I'll kill you for that—stop it—oh, help me, help me, for God's sake, won't somebody help me?" Marion shrieked. With all her might she lunged this way and that, trying to jerk her ankles against the confining pinions, dragging on her tractioned wrists, while her beautiful bare breasts jiggled and danced in the most delicious choreography.

The skirt was exceptionally full, and besides this she wore two attractive lawn petticoats. When I had grasped all this bulky fabric in my left hand and lofted it up to her waist, I found to my rising excitement the vulnerable target of her loins and bottom sheathed in dainty lace-trimmed pink silk drawers, whose legs reached nearly to mid-thigh and whose snugness shaped out the plump prominence of her Mount of Venus. I even fancied I could see the thick bush of black silky curls which framed and shielded her luscious cunt.

"Nooo!! Let my clothes down, for God's sake. Oh, you infamous brute, you vile, despicable fiend!" Marion screamed hoarsely, beside herself to find herself in such desperate straits. She wriggled and twisted frantically, straining to clench her thighs, which of course she could not do. I kept the mass of garments lifted high and now, leaning forward, I began to stroke her shapely thighs, sheathed in black silk stockings which disappeared under the legs of her drawers. I could see the white satin-elastic sheath of her stays framing the sides of her drawers and girdling her about the waist, and I now temporarily released the uprucked mass of skirt and petticoats to use both hands in unfastening the stays, which dropped to the floor between her legs. At that she uttered another agonized shriek of indescribable fury and despair.

I felt I must, in all conscience, though I had no great love for Marion, grant her at least a gentlemanly alternative of release without force, and so, removing my hands and letting her skirt and petticoats drop down, I demanded, "If you will agree to remove all of your clothing and offer yourself to me as a sign of contrition for the wrongs you have done me, Marion, I will let you down from the ropes and treat you with that kind of honor that a man accords a woman who willingly yields herself."

"Oh my God, you must be raving mad!" was Marion's hoarse, almost shouted reply, and she glared at me as vindictively as she had from the very outset. "I will give you no satisfaction, you hideous monster, you blackguard, you debaucher of innocent and helpless women!

Oh God, why did not my poor deranged sister tell me of your cowardly and perverted nature? What hypnotic coercion did you use to force her to your bestial desires?"

"Better and better," I complimented her in jest. "For this abhorrence of yours for me is almost genuine. As such, it is a challenge I cannot gainsay. You have asked a question, and I shall give you an answer. Yes, Marion, I propose to use on you those same methods of hypnotic coercion, as you so picturesquely term them, that I used on sweet Alice. Then you will be in a fair way to make honest comparisons, which will, I trust, prevent you in the future from jumping to malicious and mendacious conclusions. I am going to strip you, my beauty, and I am going to get to the very roots of you. You may prepare yourself!"

With this, despite her frenzied cries and struggles, I pitilessly rose and, seizing the rent folds of her frock, gave an energetic yank that tore the fine material down to the very hems, so that the tattered frock hung loosely around her shuddering and straining body. I found the drawstrings of the petticoats and loosened them, although of course, because of the slight spread of her lower legs, they remained clinging to her lower limbs.

The scissors were deftly applied to them and in a few minutes, all these garments festooned her as she stood exposed to me now in the magnificent deshabille of drawers, stockings and shoes, with her upper body slightly covered only by the unbuttoned blouse and bodice that yawned on either side to bare the tempting glories of her warm olive-skinned breasts.

She began to cry out for help in a hoarse, agonized voice, throwing herself this way and that, making her naked bosom globes dance and jiggle in the most lascivious manner. My prick could not stand such excitement without a further respite, for it bulged out of my dressing gown in all its stiff and inflamed virility. So once again I seated myself and tried to regain my composure, for I had no intention of hastening the conquest of this beautiful virago. Meanwhile she hung there in her bonds, panting and gasping, her face crimson and damp with sweat, her nostrils shrinking and flaring erratically, staring at me as if I were the very Devil himself, an attitude of fearful respect which I, for one, found most appropriate to the occasion!

"Now that is better," I at last commented in a clam, composed tone which told me I had at last succeeded in regaining mastery over myself and that I could proceed with full dignity and calculation to the conquest of Marion's tasty and most secret charms. "With all of that oppressive clothing removed, you are not likely to get so heated, and you are therefore much more suitably prepared to appreciate the nature of my hypnotic coercion."

"I will kill you for this, you monster!" she murmured, flashing me a savage look of undisguised look of hatred.

I can assure you, dear reader, that far from wishing to accede to her murderous desire, I had every intention of living a good long while, or at least so long as I could do justice to the mouthwatering treasures which Marion so unwillingly displayed before me. Now I could really appreciate the gracious and ample contours of her voluptuously mature body. A good inch taller than my sweet Alice, she was magnificently formed. Her thighs were somewhat longer than Alice's, and gradually rounding as they neared the appetizing hemispheres of her bottom. Her calves were sleek and rather sinuous, beautifully muscled and sculptured in the tight cling of her black silk stockings. Her knees were delightfully dimpled and suavely rounded. Going behind her for a moment to appraise her bottom, which portion of a woman's anatomy has always given a special impetus to my erotic passions,

I was entranced to find that her posterior was in some ways even more exciting in conformation than sweet Alice's. The cheeks were broadly oval and highset, with a flair and jut to the summits that was absolutely impudent and audacious. The sinuous furrow that separated them widened at the base to suggest a most delicious access to both her sexual orifices, only one of which I knew to be virgin—or at least, guessed it to be as much. Also there was a wonderfully sensual mobility to that backside of hers, for as she sensed me behind her and contemplating her, Marion tightened her sphincter muscles with a supreme effort, making the full oval globes flex and contract lasciviously, as she tried to diminish the contours of her luscious posterior and to defend herself against both gaze and touch.

Standing behind her, at last I reached out and around her to cup the delicious lovegourds of her bosom and to pinch the nipples between thumbs and forefingers. As I expected, Marion gave a shriek and lunged and twisted, but I stood up close and I felt her resiliant bottom grind and rub against my belly and loins, further agitating my aching prick until the sensation of lust was almost insupportable. Violent shuddering spasms wrenched her voluptuous body as she fought to disengage her naked bosom from my profaning clutches. The smell of her body was equally exciting to me; she had used a delicate verbena perfume, and coupled to it was the aphrodisiacal scent of sweat and of female flesh to which clung, also, the scented odor of her clothing. I detected a fine sachet. And this compound of both artificial and natural bodily effluvia whetted me as my nostrils savoringly drank it in.

Now my hands glided down her naked sides and towards the front of her drawers and, finally, to my indescribable delight, I had one palm right over Marion's cunt! Oh, how plump and enticing it was through this single thickness of fabric! My other hand rested on her inner left thigh, and I could feel the flexions of her muscles in fierce protest against my sullying touch of the most private portion of her delicious anatomy.

"Take your filthy hand away from my person—oh my God, you beast, you contemptible swine!" she panted. She jerked her bottom back to remove her front from my attack, only to feel the prodding jab of my swollen cock right up against the cleft between her bottomcheeks. She was between Scylla and Charybdis, on the very horns of a Democlean dilemma and she realized it at once, for as she felt the rude jab of my enraptured prick against her scantily sheathed bottom, Marion plunged forward again with a wailing cry: "Aaaahhh! For God's sake, no—don't shame me like this—you brute, you monster, you shameless blackguard!"

"For one who was about to apologize in the most contrite manner, my dear Marion," I told her, "you seem to have renounced that temporary humility and determined once again to defy me. Good—I accept your challenge gladly. Do you feel where my hand is, Marion! Did your husband ever caress you thus in the privacy of your conjugal chamber?" and with this I pressed my hand tightly over the prominent Mount of Venus. You cannot imagine the sensations I derived therefrom; not only the bliss of realizing that haughty Marion was at least completely in my power, mine to do with as I chose, hers to endure what I chose to inflict—but also the physical awareness of her womanhood. Oh, she was abundantly fleeced! I could feel the mass of silky curls right under the thin material of her drawers, and I knew those curls must hide the bower of her most intimate femininity.

I could no longer control my lustful urge to see those supreme charms of hers completely unveiled, and so I at-

71

tacked the tapes of her drawers which were quite tightly knotted as if in advance she had determined to provide her loins with the most infrangible of barriers.

"Oh, no don't—Oh merciful God, you can't intend to do that—Oh God, come and help me—somebody help me—he's going to ruin me!" she shrieked aloud. It was almost ludicrous, this call of hers for help, this declaration of her dreaded "ruination." From a virgin I would have expected it as a normal reaction to the initiation into the sweet mysteries of fucking; but Marion had been married for three years and could not, surely, boast of having retained her maidenhead. Or—sudden, titillating hypothesis—had she actually held off a man of normal appetites with every marital right to gratify them by denying him access to this furry niche on which my palm pressed so greedily? I paid no attention to her shrieks and clamorous cries, and I let her struggle and twist and wrench herself about all she chose while I concentrated on the unknotting of those drawstrings which denied my eyes and hands and cock the accessibility to both of her womanly grottoes.

At last I felt them yield, and I grasped the tops and then rolled them downwards with a single husking jerk. "Aaahhh! Oh, dear God in heaven—no, stop it, you hateful brute—let me go!" Marion hysterically screamed, turning her congested face back over one shoulder as if to appeal to me for mercy. Her drawers had been tugged down just below her buttocks and would go no further, owing to the slight spread of her writhing, stockinged legs. Oh, magnificent vista, the olive-smooth, warm satiny resilience of her naked bottom, those two full oval cheeks tightening now as poor Marion sought to dissemble her nakedness from my blazing eyes, from my perfidious, searching fingers! The ambery-shadowy cleft almost disappearing in this supreme contraction of her

72

bottom muscles, Marion, lunging and twisting, tried frenziedly to break her bonds and get free from what was in store for her!

Her bottom was absolutely breathtaking in its configuration and its satiny smoothness. It possessed a mobility, an agility and a musculature which promised the most lubricious joys under the assailing onslaught of my possesion of her flesh. There was at her chinkbone a most adorable kind of dimple, so that the prominent jut of the buttocks became that much more accentuated. But before I tortured myself further with palpating the naked flesh of her behind, I must see her cunt, I told myself. And so, stepping around her, pushing back to the chair, I devoured her with my gaze while her face, scarlet and contracted, glistening with beads of agony and shame-sweat, the haughty blackhaired sister of my beloved Alice writhed and groaned in a tumult of distraught emotions. Yes, it was as I had surmised: the plump triangulated aperture of her cunt was completely covered with a thick forest of glossy, silky black curls which extended from the lower abdomen and grew in profusion right over the lips of her delicious snatch, disappearing below the orifice and doubtless growing along the intimate and humid connecting groove which led to her nether slit! Words cannot describe the exquisitely salacious picture Marion made with her silk drawers rucked down just under that appetizing cunt, stretched by the slight spread of her shaking stockinged thighs, with the sweet, delicately rounded goblet of her belly adorably marked by that tempting kiss-nook which was the navel.

I was shuddering with desire and my eyes were blazing. Alice's cunt was full and plump and fleshy and prominent, but that of her sister had, shall I say, an even more seductive allure for me. At first glance, even though the thick black curls concealed its conformation, it appeared that the outer labia were somewhat more pronounced and also that the aperture was deeper than sweet Alice's tender slit. I now placed my left palm on her naked hip, and Marion started convulsively as if she had been touched with a redhot poker, uttering a wild gasp: "Ohh no, for God's sake, no Don't touch me, you horrid villain! Kill me—kill me instead!"

"But that would be punishment in great excess of what you really deserve, my beloved sister-in-law to be," I jested. "No, Marion, I promise you that you shall be kept alive, and that you will never be more alive in all your life than during the next hour or so. Ah, I see that nature has given you as protective a veil as that which you selected in your choice of attire. But let us see just how hardy it is against the siege of my eager fingers."

With this, I applied my right forefinger to the thicket of jet-black curls and Marion, with a wild scream, lunged her bare bottom backwards in a futile attempt to evade my profanation. But the first touch I had of those thick ringlets made my cock throb with elysian anticipation. Thick though they were, they had a softness and curliness to them that bespoke an absolute treasure trove of Venus beneath their protective foliage. My left hand moved round to palm her naked bottom over both cheeks, bridging the shadowy gap which separated their contracting hemispheres, and thus I could force her back to the peregrinations of my invading finger. She glanced back at that ungentlemanly hand, then once again dragged with all her strength on her wrist bonds, while tremor after tremor rippled through her tractioned body. For a moment I was playfully content to press my forefinger here and there over the large mound and to feel the thick silky curls of that delectable quim. But now the time had come to explore her innermost secrets. And so, leaning forward in my chair, my left palm pressing hard against her naked, squirming posterior, forcing her to thrust out her loins willy-nilly, I began to probe with the tip of my searching finger. Just as I had imagined, the exquisite fleshy fig of Marion's cunt was much deeper than Alice's. The outer lips formed a soft gash in that lovely mound, and they were as yet dry—a condition which I meant soon enough to alter—but deliciously crinkly-soft to my discriminating touch.

As my fingertip brushed that sensitive outer gateway which led to Marion's lovechannel, she uttered a low, sobbing groan, twisting her face to this side and then the other, her eyes tightly closed and her fists tightly clenched, but the trembling of her jaw and the flaring of her nostrils told me that she was not at all impervious to what she was experiencing. Her breasts too entered into this tumultuous anguish, thrusting out with panting exhalations, and her stentorous breathing gave the lie utterly to her attempt at stoic indifference. To my great delight, as my finger passed slowly all along that delicious aperture, first at the base of the outer lips and up to the top, then down the other lip to the base where it joined its sweet sister, I felt the membrane twitch and flutter and quiver. Oh no, Marion, for all her prudery and prim *hauteur*, was by no means the stone statue of righteousness she fancied herself!

"You coward, to try to avenge yourself in this disgusting, bestial way," she suddenly flung at me in a voice that was choked with rancor and sobs.

I blithely ignored this outburst, and I proceeded to tickle the outer lips of that soft pink chalice relentlessly back and forth, till gradually I could feel them twitch and tremor and flutter almost uncontrollably, until I could hear Marion's gasps and whimpering moans exude more frequently from between her clenched lips, and until I felt the spasmodic tightenings of her bottom muscles and the squirming, restless, uneasy movements of her naked behind against my restraining left palm.

Slyly then, I probed deeper, and I found the smaller, more delicate and slightly moist lips of the inner membrane which led to the vaginal sheath, the furrow down which at not too far distant a moment I knew my raging prick must needs surfeit its hungers for her tasty womanflesh.

Chapter 6

Just above the inner lips, my forefinger moved to discover the nodule of her clitoris, that fleshy little jewel, that lodestone, that kernel of passion which was the key to all Marion's womanly emotions and which should unlock the door to all her portals, no matter how much she fought to retain her defensive frigidity against my "abhorred" advances, and the prospect of my mastery and domination.

As my fingertip touched this tender morsel, Marion uttered a stifled groan, her head falling back, her eyes wide and exhorbitant and her nostrils flaring delicately as a feverish spasm swept her entire body. Her body shook under the shock of this impulsion, and my left palm felt the convulsive jerk of the agile muscles under the satiny skin of her naked bottom. To distract her a little, I withdrew my left hand and suddenly ran it up under the leg of her rucked-down drawers, to find the stocking top. I detected the tight and flouncy rosette garter high on her thigh which kept the black silk sheath in such impeccably unwrinkled caress of her long, shapely leg. Plucking it out, I snapped it wickedly, and drew a startled little cry of "Ohh! d-don't!" and a convulsive wriggling that made my cock jump with savage ecstasy. Again my right forefinger pressed against the nodule of her love-button, pressing it back into its protective cowl of soft, pink, protective loveflesh, then releasing it so it could bob up. This maneuver also produced a whimpering gasp and a convulsive twist from the frantic, helpless beauty, and she restlessly turned her face from side to side, her eyes again closed, her lips grimaced to show her clenched yet chattering teeth.

Now my finger withdrew, but only to attack the inner lips of her cunt again and to rim them with soft, tickling caresses, round and round, till I felt them fairly open and twitch and quiver in the insidious attunement which indisputably showed that for all her faults and her profession of disdainful contempt for the male animal, Marion was very much a warmblooded female.

"You are extremely sensitive, it would appear," I told her, forcing my hoarsening voice to remain mockingly calm, to show her she could expect no wavering or indecision from me. "I wonder if your husband must have utilized this hypnotic coercion, again to borrow your very graphic phrase, to bring you down from your aloof and untouchable pedestal."

"Damn you, damn you for your brutal, vulgar and vicious conduct to me, a helpless woman," she panted. And now she tried desperately to clench her thighs and wrench herself backwards away from my probing finger. I still had my left hand on her upper thigh, and I now snapped her garter viciously, stinging her tender flesh and drawing an anguished little "Oww—oww! End this —end this horror! Haven't you had revenge enough, you dirty brute?"

"I have hardly begun to wipe out your first sarcastic remark this afternoon, my charming sister-in-law to be," was my answer.

I now felt it necessary to call a momentary halt to the proceedings, because my plans had somewhat altered for the subjugation of Alice's sister. Marion was, after all, twenty-seven, two years older than Alice; and where Alice had been a virgin, Marion most assuredly could not be after three years of marriage. Yet to this point, though I had already stripped her and felt her a good deal, I had not actually ascertained her true hymeneal status, and this I meant to do forthwith. Moreover, Marion had grossly insulted and injured me and therefore deserved a sterner reprisal than I had given her delicious sister for holding me off yet still tantalizing me. No, I had steeled my heart; Marion should not be reprieved into receiving any of the tender and creature comforts which I had bestowed on Alice.

She stood there shuddering and groaning, her face turned to one side, resolute in her intention not to look at me and continuing her ridiculous ostrich-like attitude of trying to banish all this unpleasantness from her mind.

So, finally pushing the chair backwards, I knelt down and clasped her slim ankles in the black silk hose, and gradually ran my hands upwards, gently squeezing the fine calves and kneehollows and thighs. While Marion cried out hysterically for help, and made the most violent contortions which her bonds permitted to try to close her thighs against my amorous inroads. She was closer to her moment of truth than she knew, for the sight of her in this scandalous half-nakedness had inflamed me even more than the stripping of her sister had done, very possibly because of her resistance and defiance and continued arrogance.

"From the way you carry on, Marion," I said cruelly, "you would have me believe you to be an untouched, blushing, shy virgin who is ready to faint dead away at the first lustful touch of a man. Now I cannot credence this after three years of marriage, even though they terminated unhappily. I must therefore determine for myself what your marital condition bestowed upon you. In a word, my charming sister-in-law to be, I am going to see whether you still retain your maidenhead."

A look of horror passed over her face now as she stared down at me, her nostrils furiously dilating and shrinking, her lips trembling, and finally in a husky, stifled voice she panted, "I see that I am helpless now and that, cowardly dog that you are, you are determined to abuse me. Very well, I cannot prevent it, but I warn you that you shall pay dearly for what you have done to me. Oh, God, if I only had a brother or my husband to avenge me, you would be dead now!"

I did not reply to his, for I was staring eagerly at her cunt. The thick, abundant black curls which covered it themselves gave me no clue as to her sexual nature, but I now passed my right forefinger against the center of that hidden grotto and pressed it on between the fleshy outer lips of Marion's pleasure channel. She caught her breath and tilted back her head, her eyes desperately closed as tightly as she could get them, and her body went rigid. It was a magnificent spectacle to observe how the muscles of her sleek calves, so beautifully and provocatively sheathed in the clinging black silk stockings, flexed and trembled from the nervous stress upon her system in this beleaguered pose. I paid no heed to it except to constate it as a further proof that she would have me believe her immaculate and untouched ere this. And I foraged my finger onward, past the smaller inner labia of her slit, till I felt myself intrude within that tender mysterious groove which nature has afforded for the gratification of my sex. Up to the hilt I plunged my finger, and I looked up triumphantly: she was decidedly no virgin!

Her teeth were chattering again, and all her muscles were in mobile tension as she stood there, stiffened and quivering with baffled fury and shame. Once again her olive cheeks were dyed a flaming scarlet hue, and the pulse-hollow in her aristocratic throat was even more visibly hammering from her agitated senses.

Whisking my finger out of her cunt, I straightened before her, and I boldly cupped her breasts, tickling her nipples with the tips of my forefingers as I stared into her congested face. My cock prooded against the silky hairs of her mount; and, sucking in her breath again very sharply, Marion executed a violent, convulsive recoiling with the intent of placing her most vulnerable niche at a distance from my person. "So," I gloatingly remarked, "you are not quite the blushing maiden you would have me believe you to be. Now how is it that after three years of supposedly blissful conjugal relations, you decided to dispense with your husband? Can it be that he did not know how to satisfy your true secret passions, Marion?"

"Ohhh!!" It would be impossible to describe the horrified tone with which she pronounced this expletive. And for a moment, her large eyes opened and inflicted upon me a withering, raging look. Yes, I had hurt Marion in her secret woman's pride, I had implied that this haughty and patrician goddess had feet of clay and could not hold her man. I had impugned the most intimate part of her life, but you will observe that I had rather placed the blame on her husband than on her, lasciviously suggesting that her lusts were inordinate, whereas my belief was that it was quite the other way around and that very likely Marion was a deficient lover to the point where her husband had sought his amorous diversions elsewhere.

"Well," I continued, for I nad now determined to carry on this delightful little ruse, "I will try my humble best to satisfy your desires, Marion. At the same time, my method should acquaint you with the capabilities I have for satisfying your sister whom I seriously intend to marry and this time without brooking any further interference or nastiness from you. In a word, Marion, I am going to fuck you and I am going to try to satisfy the urges which I am certain give you such an irascible temperament . . . which can only come about when a woman is not sexually satisfied!"

"No! I shan't let you—I'd rather die, you loathsome beast! Help me, Oh, for God's sake won't someone help me? You shan't have me, you shan't!" she cried in a loud hoarse voice as she flung herself this way and that against her bonds.

For answer, I unbelted my dressing-gown and slipped it off my shoulders, letting it fall behind me, and I was naked. My prick was in violent erection as you may well suppose, and the head was swollen and purplish with pent-up ardor. I stepped closer to her, and I reached round and palmed the lower cheeks of her bottom, luxuriating in the warm satiny smoothness of those impudent and resilent globes, in the frantic contractions with which all the muscles now came into play as she realized that her defeat was imminent.

Putting my lips to one of her nipples, I took it between them and nuzzled it delicately, flicking it with my tongue, and she uttered another hoarse shout, absolutely beside herself at the liberties I was taking with her fair person: "Ohh—no, no, you monster, you wretch, I don't want you to have me, I won't let you, I'd sooner die, oh let me go, you contemptible coward!"

Keeping my left palm against her quivering bare bottom, I shifted my right hand in front of us and with my forefinger I again attacked her cunt. This time, I went directly to the tender hidden lodestone of her clitoris, and I began to rub it insistently and lingeringly, making her thighs jerk convulsively with the erotic stimulus. I could see that beads of sweat were gathering in her finely downed soft armpit-hollows, and the scent of her sweat and of her naked flesh now began to overpower the artificial perfume with which she had doused herself. Her eyes rolled, her nostrils opened and closed convulsively and at a more accelerated pace, while she made a frenzied effort to clench her thighs and, of course, could not.

I cannot tell you what maddening pleasure I experience as I kept my left hand firmly pressed against her jerking, squirming, contracting naked bottom and my forefinger pressed against the nodule of her very life. And as I continued to suck and nibble at her nipple, I felt it stiffen and turgify, indisputable proof that she was, for all of her injurious and embattled behavior, a mature woman of ardent flesh and blood, quite capable of being stimulated to the point of yielding to the good fucking I meant to give her.

Now inarticulate groans exuded from her gaping mouth, as she relentlessly turned her face from side to side, and from time to time dragged mercilessly on her bound wrists. It was evident that all of her senses were now being tumultuously wakened, try as she would to deny them. She had set me a magnificent challenge, and I was extremely grateful to her!

I swore to myself that I would topple her from this pedestal of exalted aloofness and that I would make of her a more humble and willing slave than even Alice was! Moreover, I would bring Alice with me as my assistant at a not too distant day, and the two of us would proceed to indoctrinate arrogant Marrion into all the exquisite and perversely lustful pleasures that a man and a maid may take with a defiant woman!

But now the time had come for me to seek some momentary relief from the frenzied torment which I myself had suffered in this lengthy ordeal of hers. For a moment

I took my forefinger out of her cunt, letting her gasp and shudder and slowly bow her head, while long rippling tremors of enervation swept over her. The down-rucked drawers festooning the tops of her straining thighs effectively hampered her movements, but they would not prevent my penetration of her soft fleshy cunt in the least. Later, to be sure, she would be further stripped and made even more acquiescent to my desire, I savoringly promised myself.

This brief respite left her more agitated than ever, judging from the spasmodic heavings of her naked breasts. The sweet tidbit which I had sucked and nibbled at glistened with my saliva, and it was darker and stiffer, too. I had at last reached this aloof and disdainful creature and brought her to a sensual awareness of herself, though I could only speculate on what emotions were truly roused by my so doing. For I had not yet learned the reason for her husband's breaking off with her, and I assuredly meant to before the afternoon was done.

Now, releasing her bottom, I used the median and forefinger of my left hand to delve through that thick verdure and press open the fleshy outer labia of her slit, while grasping my cock exactly at the groove with my right thumb and forefinger, I advanced my savagely rigid weapon towards its goal!

As soon as she felt my fingers on her cunt, Marion uttered a wild cry and again began to struggle with all her might, wriggling backwards, twisting from side to side, wildly dragging at her tractioned wrists, turning her contorted, scarlet face in every direction as she supplicatingly besought some supreme reprieve. But this time there would be none for her!

For slowly, following her jerky spasms hither and yon in the short space which her bonds permitted, and keeping her cuntlips widely yawned apart, I at last entered my prick into the opening thus afforded, and, feeling myself well inside the outer portals of her slit, now gripped the lower curves of both buttocks with eager and sinewy fingers as I ruthlessly forced myself inside her till I was buried in her to the very balls!

Marion uttered a gurgling scream, and, in a supreme effort of contempt and maddened fury, spat fully into my face!

How I loved her at that moment, how I gloatingly savored this new and outrageously unladylike manifestation of her spleen! For now she had added not one but several fresh pages to the ledger of her account. She would be soundly punished for what she had done— after I had fucked her.

But the overpowering sensation of being inside of Alice's sister's cunt took full possession of me now. How wonderfully tight and warm she was, almost as if she were a virgin after all! I felt myself sheathed and clamped upon in her warm snatch, and I had no desire to move about, so rapt was I in tasting the myriad sensations of my sweet confinement. With my fingers digging into the cheeks of her bare behind, feeling the sporadic flexions and the quiverings of that resilent olive-satiny flesh, I once again bent my head to her other nipple now and began to suck it noisily, to embarrass and spite her, to suggest that we were the tenderest of lovers instead of the deadliest of enemies.

And when she felt that suction, the frantic jerkings which her body gave vent to provided me with the most delierious pleasure, for she was providing her own friction to my imbedded cock.

"Beast! Monstrous rapist! Filthy degenerate!" she panted in a sobbing, strangled voice. "Is this the way you overpowered my poor sister and made her your degraded slave? Oh God, if there is any justice, you will never live to boast of the bestial thing you are doing to me!"

"But again, you needlessly malign me, dear Marion," I twitted her as I pushed myself back till I was crammed inside her to the very hilt, wanting that luxuriating completeness of being thoroughly and fully housed inside her warm narrow quivering grotto. "Far from needing to force your sister, I may say that she delights in the attentions that I pay her. As I promise you that you will do before I have finished with you, my dear sister-in-law to be!"

"You selfish, vainglorious, hypocritical beast of a man!" she burst out tearfully," So smug in your belief that because you are a brutal animal, you can make a decent woman yield to you and share your ignoble, filthy pleasures! You shall have nothing of me, you shall have to force me every step of the way, I will resist, I will rebel —Owww!"

I had found it rather repetitiously boring to listen to her jeremiads and upbraiding, so I had stealthily applied my left thumb and forefinger to the base of her right buttock and inflicted a painful quick pinch, which was the reason for her sudden rather ludicrous squeal of pain and the sudden wild jerk of her naked hips, which almost unsheathed my weapon from her amorous depths.

"That, my dear Marion, is a little advance on the punishment due you for spitting at me. I perceive that you are a nasty cat and such animals must thoroughly be shown who is master." And as she writhed and groaned, I cupped both her naked breasts in my eager hands and began to suck first at one nipple and then the other, whilst arching myself forward so that every inch of my blade would be consummately burrowed in that tight warm sheath of hers. A sobbing groan responded to this new maneouver of mine, a sweet and thrilling promise

86

that haughty Marion would ultimately abandon her raging defiance and become mine as surely as her sister had become!

Chapter 7

At last I had achieved my long-dreamed-of match with haughty Marion. And yet I was a long way from having achieved full satisfaction—by that I do not mean climax, for the way her tight warm cunt clung to my imbedded cock told me that very shortly I should have to pay a tribute to her which would not be due entirely to her delicious powers, but rather to my own cumulative passion. No, the satisfaction I intended was to turn this aloof and contemptuous young matron into as submissive a love-slave as ever Alice now was . . . more than that, to make her humbly beg pardon for having so insulted and perjured me, to say nothing of the slap and the spittle which had been her tender gifts to me thus far. And even beyond that, I foresaw that I would have Alice and her lovely maid Fanny, and possibly even lovely Connie Blunt participate in a fucking and feathering and frigging fray wherein Marion would be the *piece de resistance*.

She had, to be sure, adopted the only possible attitude for herself; totally helpless, arms dragged high above her head, legs slightly spread and ankles tethered by the silken ropes to the opposing wallrings, she had tried first the ostrich trick of pretending that this was not happening to her, and now finally she had resorted to furiously defiant bravado, warning me of my demise for the great affront I had done her. She had not even begun to know the full measure of my capacity for subjugation.

For I wished her to enjoy the subtle psychological nuances of her own defeat as thoroughly as I now meant to enjoy her voluptuous, olive-skinned loveliness. To conquer her flesh was only half the battle, therefore.

I paused once again, grinding my teeth to hold back the sudden spasmodic urge to ejaculate my boiling balsam, and I contemplated her scarlet, congested face, admiring the lascivious offertory which her yawning blouse and bodice made to expose the heaving turrets of her beautiful bare breasts. Both nipples now were stiff and wet with my saliva, and that stiffness suggested a carnal attunement which I was not yet certain she actually felt. I would bring her to it, never fear!

"You are extremely tight to my fit," I now mockingly observed as my fingers sank into the quivering hillocks of her behind. "I ask myself, dear Marion, whether this presupposes an infrequency of pleasure between yourself and your so-recently departing husband. Can it be that he neglected you and did not perform his marital duties as often you would have liked?"

At this she stiffened and uttered a low, sobbing groan, twisting her face far to one side to avoid me, and I felt her trembling against me. You cannot imagine the fluttering, delicious sensations directed against my rutting prick by those tremors of her body which almost felt as if they came from her vaginal sheath itself. I realized also that her long sojourn in this vertical position which imposed such pitiless upward traction on her arms must by now be extremely irksome for her, but in no way did I feel tenderhearted enough to grant her mercy as I had done with Alice when I had allowed my sweet beloved to take her fucking on the couch.

Of course, to be perfectly truthful about that first

glorious affair with the sisters, I must admit that Alice had not initially come to the couch at first of her own free will, for I had had at first to tie her over the stool and apply the whip smartly to her hindquarters to compel her obedience, after which I had bottomfucked her. Only then had she realized the uselessness of further struggles and decided to cast herself on my tender mercies and make the most—or actually the best!—of her situation.

But Lady Marion—or so I ironically termed her in my mind—should not have any such concessions. Her account was long overdue and it was by now far in excess of its original debt. I meant to humiliate her and shame her all I could, because by moral and mental suffering alone would it be possible to strip away this hypocritical smugness and holier-than-thou veneer with which she had cloaked herself so effectively.

Drawing my cock out to the very brink of her warm slit, while my fingers luxuriantly pinched and squeezed her bare bottom cheeks, I pursued my taunting interrogation: "No, I think we may both admit on good authority that you were not a virgin when you came to me this afternoon, by dear Marion, and so let us both seek to analyze what it was that drove your husband away and give me this golden opportunity to be alone with you in this cherished intimacy!"

"Oh, you vicious, unprincipled dog, you wretched scoundrel!" she suddenly groaned, and blinked her large dark blue eyes, full of sudden tears, "it is no affair of yours, you monster, you demon! Yes, have your pleasure now, for I can't defend myself because of your vicious cowardice, but my turn will come, I swear it will! When the judge pronounces sentence upon you for your vile rape and disgusting treatment of a decent woman, then it will be your turn to quail."

"I rather doubt that you will prefer charges against me, my dear sister-in-law to be," was my reply as I gave her a nasty little pinch at the base of a jouncy bottom cheek by dint of squeezing thumb and forefinger together, making her squeal and wriggle in the most delightful way—which of course further rasped the tender lining of her amorous fissure against my hilted cock. "It would be your word against mine, and I may say that I have some fair reputation in the City and good acquaintanceship amongst many illustrious judges and notable barristers. But more than that, my defense would be that you shamelessly came, bereft of a husband who had not been enough to satisfy your carnal needs, seeking to seduce me. And when you found you could not by your blandishments, you ragingly set upon me, spitting and slapping at me like a common shrew. Now if you would attempt to give this the lie, my charming sister-in-law to be, it would be necessary for you to go into precise and intimate detail as to my *modus operandi*. I think you far too prim and puritanical for that. So you see, Marion, you will just have to resign yourself to the punishment which you so richly have deserved."

"You blackguard! A decent woman could not—would not have the vulgarity, the shamelessness—to speak of such monstrosities as you are committing now with me!" she moaned.

"Exactly. This shall be our secret between the two of us, unless you want me to tell Alice that you sought me out here in her absence so that you could partake of the sweet pleasures which till now have been hers solely to enjoy."

"You would not do that," she suddenly gasped, and her eyes were enormous now with a shadowing fear.

Aha! I said silently to myself. Can it be that I have unwittingly stumbled upon some secret difference between these two beauties which will really solve my domestic problems in the most delicious manner? So, pursuing this line of thought, I countered: "Yes, I rather think I shall do precisely that, Marion. Alice is likely to be jealous, you know, and since you are the older sister, she will resent your poaching in her premises. And the more so as, as I have told you, I intend to wed your sister as soon as she will have me."

Now I will confess in all honesty that I did not have an immediate intention of espousing my beautiful Alice, but I also hasten to add as a gentleman that it was not because I had already tasted her charms and known her favors. She was not any less desirable for all of that. No, it was simply that I had enjoyed my freedom all these years, and it gave me an inordinate sense of well-being and masterry to remain free of shackles and to proceed with a delicious woman like Alice as if I were the lord and she the concubine and quivering slave. However, it seemed to me that if I played my cards well this afternoon I might well achieve the most incredibly rewarding and complex of relationships for let us say that I did wed Alice and now fully conquered her sister, would I not have two harem beauties to my beck and call? This mental process almost unnerved me to the point of losing all my gism, and it was only with a supreme effort that, grinding my teeth and closing my eyes, I could force back the furious ejaculation rising in my testicles. It was salacious enough to conduct such a heated conversation with a beautiful young matron who was practically naked and bound to my desires, so salacious indeed that the mental awareness of it alone was enough to produce loss of control.

"Sir, I implore you, if you have any mercy in you, say nothing to my sister—and—and—" she could not finish.

"And what, then, Marion?" I pursued. Once again I

pinched the base of her buttock to spur her to alacrity of response, and again she squealed and jerked this way and that, affording to my imbedded cock most delightful sensations.

"Aah! Oh don't, don't sir! It is dreadful to treat a woman this way, dreadful! Have you no kindness, no mercy?"

"Why? Did you expect any, after the way you stormed at me from the first moment you entered my apartment? And then after you slapped me and spit into my face? Oh no, I cannot credit you with any of the tender virtues which I most respect in womanhood," I answered. "But you have not yet answered my question: If I do not tell Alice about this little seance of ours, what will you do?"

"Have pity on me—I am so weak—I am helpless, and you are torturing me, shaming me. It's brutal and vile. Be merciful and let me go, and I swear I will forget what I said about denouncing you to the authorities," she finally quavered.

"I could not be certain of your word, Marion, since you have already broken it half a dozen times over since we entered the Snuggery," I said sternly. "No, you are going to give me full satisfaction. You are going to answer all my questions, you are going to obey my orders, and you are going to act like a woman at long last and not a creature of spells and tantrums and insolence. I do not recognize in you at all any of those sweet attributes which Alice so lovingly possesses. And to think it was you who came between us so long ago and postponed our happiness. If she were here now, Marion, I think she would want to stand here beside me and share my role of judge, jury and executioner."

This shaft struck home, to my great delight! She gasped and stared at me with tear-brimming eyes, her lips trembling feverishly, her naked breasts heaving in a tumult of agitation. Then suddenly she stammered, closing her eyes and shivering as with ague, "Oh, in God's name, you mustn't tell Alice. Oh, please, have pity on me and don't do that, sir!"

"And why not? Do I owe you anything after the way you have flouted me, after the way you appeared a year ago between Alice and myself, and even now you harbor thoughts of estranging us," I warmed to my theme which by chance shot I had so fortunately discovered. Yes, haughty Marion had her Achilles' heel after all; somehow, though till now I had not known it, there existed some kind of strained relationship between these two beauties, and much to my surprise I found that Marion was actually afraid of letting her younger sister learn about this exciting little interlude. But why?

"I know . . . I've treated you very badly. But you must understand—oh, how can you make me speak this way, tied as I am so indecently at your mercy? Let me down, sir, oh, please let me down and give me a chance to think," Marion stammered in a faint, husky voice which thrilled me to my very core. I was not yet ready to grant her this favor; I much preferred the hostile patrician who lorded it over me. To have her humbled thus suddenly was not entirely in my scheme of things. Yet I had to consider the alternatives.

Meanwhile, while she waited to learn my decision, I meant to appease the agony of my inflamed cock, which all this while had remained dug into the very vitals of her, tasting her warm, tight channel and appreciating with a savoring rapture this intimate cohesion between two people who had certainly not seemed at the outset predestined as lovers!

"I will afford you every opportunity to reveal your inscrutable nature to me, Marion, but only when I have fucked you," I told her coldy, and then sinking my

95

fingers deeply into her velvety bottomcheeks, I drew back slightly and plunged to the balls inside of her, drawing a gasp from my beautiful victim. Now my self-control somewhat deserted me. The prospect of subjecting her and bending her to my will had seemed such a remote possibility and now was unexpectedly shown to me as an immediate possibility, and it quite destroyed my carefully conjured plans. So, with a groan, after two or three more deep thrusts inside her quaking cunt, I felt myself explode and spatter her to the depth of her matrix with my bubbling juices. She gave a moaning sob at this knowledge of her sullying, and, turning her head to one side, she let the tears run down her cheeks—abject and helpless, really a pitiable object, were it not that her damnably arrogant beauty had inflamed me to think of her more as a rebellious Amazon than as a pleading and humble mistress.

I withdrew myself and repaired to the watercloset to sponge myself and make my proper ablutions. When I returned, it was to pose before her the large plate glass mirror nearly eight feet high which reflected her at full length. Stark naked, I moved to one side and studied her as she remained panting and groaning, and I could see the thick black tufts of her private hairs stickied with my copious libation to Venus. With her drawers still down just below the sweet grotto from which I had so recently emerged, with the blouse and bodice swinging open to frame for my entranced view the sight of her two dark-nippled, heaving breasts, Marion was absolutely ravishing. And now the second phase of my conquest was to begin, laying more stress on the psychological than on the physical, until I should draw from her all those secrets which as yet were denied me, so that I might taste her very marrow as no man had ever done before. Insofar as this could be done, Marion remained a virgin to me, an unknown quantity, whose unfathomed depths I meant to probe.

Chapter 8

The mirror which I had placed in front of my quivering captive was not only tall enough but also wide enough so that it would reveal me behind her. By now I meant to pass to the second phase of her ordeal, which would be in part psychological and part physical, both parts meant to punish and humble and shame her to the utmost so that she would at last reveal the real reasons for her stubbornness and apparent frigidity and haughty cruelty towards me.

In my cupboard I kept a riding whip of a soft substance which was quite springy and elastic, and which had the particular propensity of stinging but not marking the naked flesh it kissed. I also had a long globe-box in which I kept about a dozen and finely pointed feathers. Both the whip and the feathers had scored Alice off especially well, and there was no reason to suppose that they could not effect a similar subjugation of her older sister, especially as Marion had finally begun to divulge to me some hint as to the reason for her inexplicable disdain of me.

First, taking the scissors, I cut away the blouse and bodice so that she was absolutely naked down to the tops of her thighs. Then, since her drawers would be no further use to her and only an impediment to the whip as well as the feathers, I cut them off too. Marion, who seemed to be languishing there with bowed head, trembling from time to time and uttering an inarticulate sigh or two, raised her head and tried to turn her face back over one shoulder to learn what this manoeuver signified.

"You will find that mirror much more comfortable for your watching, my dear Marion," I amusedly told her. "Indeed, it will let you anticipate in advance what I am about to do to you. And the extent of this part of your ordeal, my girl, will depend to a large extent upon your willingness to be truthful with me. The absolute, the utter truth, without adulteration or faction, Marion, is what I want from you!"

Now she stood only in those black silk stockings high along her beautiful thighs, with flouncy rosette garters holding them up on her lovely long legs. Otherwise, she was magnificently naked, and the olive sheen of her bare flesh, the deep chiseled hollow of the supple back, seemed all the more alluring and libidinously enticing against the contact which those stockings made.

And now that she was thus naked, I could feast my eyes undeterred upon her charms and compare her with her sister. Alice's legs were, as I have already remarked, the least trifle too short for her, but this very defect had added to the indescribable fascination of her figure. Alice had plump and round thighs which tapered to the neatest of calves and ankles, and tiny patrician feet. Her waist was dainty but not too small, and she had fine rounded arms with small well-shaped hands. The magnificent curves of hips and haunches, the graciously swelling belly with its deep navel, and the full, fat, fleshy and prominent mount of love together with her rather full, firm and outstanding bubbies, made her really mouthwatering. Yet Marion was visibly more mature, and, slightly taller—she seemed taller still because of the

100

traction of the wrist ropes—which added further to her seductiveness. The jouncy, spacious ovals of her naked bottom fairly invited the whip as well as pinches and slaps, and the beautifully pronounced curve of her back and the dimple at her chinkbone which marked that beginning of the sinous, shadowy groove separating her superb buttocks set my cock to aching all over again. It would not be long before Marion would be called upon to service me, and this time in a more leisurely and thorough way than the first fuck had been. For when a man initially conquers a beautiful, defiant and spirited girl, the excitement of the procedure very often defeats him, and he cannot withhold himself to make the conquest so complete as he would like. This had been the case with me, as I have just narrated, for the feeling of my prick inside Marion's choice, haughty and seemingly unattainable cunt had overcome even my own excellent staying powers. But now that the first furious libation to Venus had been poured out, I knew that I would be easily able to prolong my pleasure with this brownhaired beauty.

The first step, now that I had stripped her except of hose, which I meant her to keep for the sake of contrast and voluptuous naughtiness (a draped female, no matter if she wears only stockings, is infinitely more prick-hardening than a totally nude girl), would be the psychological one. Now, her attire in visiting me had been so voluminous and so overly modest as to let me suppose that she was untouchable, unattainable and far above my unworthy person. And since these had been stripped away and her act as a *poseur* found out, I wished to alter her coiffure, for it too symbolized her very disdain of me.

As I moved behind her, I saw that she was glancing in the mirror, and that her eyes were very wide and her lips parted, that she almost was leaning forward a little as if

101

to perceive what I meant to do to her next. This was an admirable state of mind, and I therefore did not hurry. The first danger was over; she had as much as retracted her furious threats of having me incarcerated in prison for my "rape" of her. Well, it was not really a rape. But there were curious circumstances concerning Marion's attitude which needed explanation. This second phase of my endeavors against her would provide precisely that.

Now her coiffure added an ambiguity which exactly indicated the duel nature of Marion's personality. Along the top of her high forehead was that little fringe of frilly curls, which suggested a saucy, rather coy girlishness, an almost juvenile ingenuousness. Yet at the back of her stately head, the mass of her glossy black hair was fixed into an exaggeratedly large oval-shaped bun, which I had already remarked on as resembling a kind of crown. That portion of her coiffure indicated her innate and insolent wish to dominate and to "lord it over" even her betters. And that was why I at last reached up both hands and began to unknot that arrogant crown.

Once again I had hit home directly. For Marion started, uttered a husky sobbing "Ohh, what are you doing to me now, you villian?" after perceiving my action in the mirror in front of her, then tried to turn her head. I gave her hair a little yank and rudely told her, "Hold still unless you want to feel pain. And since you have called me villian and blackguard and scoundrel often enough in the short time you have spent here, I may as well have the game as well as the name."

This momentarily quelled her, but when she saw me loosen her hair and rumple it out with my fingers till it fell in a rich ebony cascade to her shoulderblades, she caught her breath again and closed her eyes and bowed her head in resignation. Decidedly I had attacked her vulnerability this time. And now there was a wonderful femininity and grace to her which she had not had before. Now she was more softly alluring and not quite so harshly embittered. And more than ever, now, being able to adapt my own views as circumstances changed and altered, I resolved that I would make Marion my passionate, complaisant mistress while marrying her sister and thus having to myself a secret harem of infinite quality. There would also be Fanny, Alice's lovely maid, and delicious Connie Blunt. The future prospect was dazzlingly bright indeed!

I stood there for a long moment behind her, with my cock in full erection, my hands on my hips, as if pondering her fate. Actually, I had long since decided on it, but this pause was purposely chosen to agonize her, to heighten her suspense, to weaken her nervous resistance to the point where she would be frantically willing to grant me what I yearned of from her tasty olive-tinted, vibrant flesh.

For openers, I now passed my hands round and in front of her, grabbing her beautiful bubbies and squeezing them lingeringly, while I moved up close behind her so that the tip of my aching cock just brushed the base of her behind and suggestively prodded the warm, slightly humid furrow that divided that magnificent posterior. Once again Marion caught her breath and stiffened, uttering a long, heartrending sigh. And she also closed her eyes, so that she would not have to be shamed by watching my sinewy strong fingers close like tentacles over her swelling, glorious breasts!

"Are you feeling a little more humble now, dear sister-in-law to be?" I sarcastically demanded. I felt her bottom twitch and contract against my gently, slyly, prodding cocktip, and I stared over her right shoulder to follow her reactions in the hugh mirror placed before her. A wave of scarlet suffused her lovely haughty face, and her chin was trembling as she bit her lips, not able to answer. I tightened my fingers over those luscious bubbies, and I hissed "You are going to have to learn to answer me when I ask you a question, Marion, or take the consequences! Now, what do you say?"

"Oh, please—my b—b—breasts—they—they're very sensitive—please don't hurt them like that—I—Ohh, s—sir, I—I already told you I—I'm sorry I did what I did. I should have left and not argued with you—but you were so hateful! Oh please, now that you've had your revenge, won't you let me go and hide my shame? You—you have my word I won't inform on you!"

The low, vibrant and tremblingly husky voice in which she expressed this supplication was really amusing to my ears. Exactly why she changed so quickly from the spiteful and furiously threatening happy to the pleading, acquiescent captive?

"That was not exactly a direct answer, but it will do for the moment," I coldly told her. "Now, why are you so intent upon my not acquainting Alice with our little *tête-à-tête* this afternoon?"

Now the large dark blue eyes did open, and she groaned and then tried to turn her face round to look at me, while I kept my fingers tightened over her heaving titties. "You mustn't—oh give me your word—I'll keep mine—please, please, sir, be merciful! I would die of shame if Alice ever knew that I've allowed you such liberties—"

"Evidently it causes you great chargrin. But why? I insist on knowing, and that is what you are going to tell me. Or shall I pinch your nipples—thus?" and, suiting action to word, I made pincers of my thumbs and forefingers and plucking out her darkened stiffened nipples from their coral centers, I insidiously squeezed.

"Aiiii! Ohh, don't, don't, for God's sake, let go of them!

Oh please, I'll tell you what you want to know, but please don't pinch me there!" she wailed.

"Then speak before I lose my patience with you, Marion!" I commanded.

Bowing her head, and in a voice choking with sobs, she stammered, "I—I've always been a sort of older aunt to Alice, you s—see, and I was first to marry and I thought I'd made a catch. I boasted to Alice, even when I soon learned that—well, that I had made a mistake. But I was too proud to admit it. And then, when I first heard that she was infatuated with you, sir, I—I resolved that she should not have the chance to c—compare, as it were."

"Now we are getting to the heart of the matter. I commend you for your veracity so far. And now you are going to tell me precisely why you learned you had made a mistake. Yet you spent three years with this man, did you not?"

Again she bowed her head, and her face turned a furious scarlet from forehead to throat. Her eyes closed, her eyelashes fluttering, and with a great effort she managed to stammer in a low and trembling voice, "Oh, sir, if you've any mercy at all for me, have pity on my shame and—and don't ask me to tell you that. Please—please be content with—with what you've had of me and let me be now."

For answer, while I kept my left thumb and forefinger at her nipple, I plunged my right hand down to the furry moss of her cunt and, and, plucking a sprig of silky black hair, I drew on it ominously, intimating that I was ready to yank it out by the roots. "The truth, Marion!" I insisted and gave it a tiny tug.

"Owww!! Oh don't, not there, oh I couldn't stand it, oh please have mercy, I'll tell, I'll tell!" she cried hysterically, trying to maneuver her tethered body so as to ease the tension on her sensitive pussyhair. Without relaxing my grip, I countered. "Then speak at once, or I will pluck it out. You are much too well protected in that area anyway."

Her bubbies rose and fell with violent turbulence now, as, head bowed, eyes tightly shut, Marion vouchsafed in her husky, tear-filled voice the explanation which I had been so curiously eager to possess: "He—he was ten years older than I, and very wealthy and, I had heard considered quite a distinguished gentleman. Our parents died when we were young, and an elderly aunt brought us up till we were about nineteen. She left only a little money for us, and Alice is so extravagant at times, you've no idea—"

I gave the sprig of silky private hair another encouraging little yank to hasten her story.

"Oww—don't, I'm going to tell, please don't do it, please!" was the frightened outcry.

"Be quick then!" I warned, and I gave her nipple a sly little pinch which made her sob and groan and squirm about.

"I'll tell, I'm going to tell. Oh, please don't hurt me—you see, I wanted security, and he had so much to offer. And I thought, well, it would mean money for Alice to buy fine clothes and things she liked, too and I did admire him, I truly did at first."

"Well, what happened to change your rosy outlook?"

"He—he revealed his true colours on our w-wedding n-night," she faltered, again averting her face and keeping her eyes closed while her blushes continued to flame on that soft olive skin of hers. "I—I had been a virgin till then, and I was proud of it. And I was shy, but he behaved like an animal. He—he practically tugged off my clothes, and I started to cry, and he laughed at me as being a silly girl much too old for such vapors. And then he—he h-had me. And it hurt a good deal and there—wasn't any p-pleasure in it."

"Was it always that way during your marriage?"

She nodded with a sniffle. "Nearly always. But after about a year, he grew weary of my pleading with him to be more tender and considerate. He—he kept a girl in a flat in Soho, I found out. And then he seduced my young maid Lucille. I—I found them together one afternoon when I came back from shopping earlier than expected. He only laughed at me and told me if I wouldn't give him what he wanted, he knew where he could get it. I held out only because I didn't want the disgrace of ending our marriage right away. And for Alice's sake, too. I knew that he would have to make a settlement when the marriage was over. And—and now you know. And I've never even told Alice. She's thought me flighty or too particular, but she didn't know. And I thought you—you were a brute the way he was."

It had truly been an amazing afternoon, though it was far from being over! From a raging leopard, my beautiful blackhaired sister-in-law to be had turned into a trembling lamb. And I confess that I felt a little synpathy for her now which she had not previously deserved. Only an inconsiderate brute would have tried to force such a magnificent figure of a woman when with patience and voluptuous skill he could have exacted from her what I already had and would still more.

"Very well, Marion," I said at last." I shall not give away your story, and it will be our secret. But all the same, my girl, I cannot let you off scot-free after the wicked tantrum you displayed in slapping me and spitting at me. You have alienated my admiration and potential affection for you by such ill-bred manners, and you must agree to accept your punishment for this naughtiness before I can relent and seek a new start with you as your brother-in-law to be."

She drew a long shuddering breath, lifted her head, then bowed it, and then, while my cockhead lightly nuzzled at the shadowy groove between her luscious bare bottomcheeks, falteringly responded: "If only you will give me your word that you won't tell Alice, then I will submit myself. But what else could I think, sir, when you went at me so brutally? It was like Harry all over again."

"He never once gave you pleasure in all the time he made love to you?" I demanded.

She shook her head, her blushes deepening.

"Well, he was a fool, and you were a greater fool to tolerate him for three years." I harshly stated. "So after all I did not lie to you when I wrote you that note saying that I had information involving your future happiness. For, Marion, I propose in the time ahead of us to initiate you into the unknown mysteries of passion which will surely gratify you as much as they will me. But you must make up your mind that there will be also some pain, and that will be your punishment. Do you agree to this?"

"What—what else can I do, s—sir?" she faintly quavered.

As I released the soft curly sprig of intimate hair, I put my forefinger boldly through the mossy fur and touched the petulant fleshy lips of her cunt, and I said: "Now you are showing wisdom. And in due course I will show you the mercy you have implored."

So saying, I went to the cupboard and procured the glove-box of feathers and the springy whip, and resumed my place behind her. Taking up the whip first, I put my left hand to the back of her neck, and I demanded,

"When you and Alice went to school, Marion, were you ever birched or caned?"

"N—no, o—only on my hands once," she said in a faint trembling voice.

"Suppose," I pursued ironically," "You had slapped your teacher? How many strokes do you think you should have received then?"

"Oh dear!" she groaned, "More than I could bear, I'm sure of it!"

"And then if you had spat in her face—"

"Oh please, don't torture me so! If—if you must have your revenge, take it, while I still have the courage to endure it! But if you only knew how uncomfortable I am, how all my limbs ache, you would show kindness and put an end to it," she sobbed.

"Very well, I shall pronounce sentence. For the slap, eight good cuts with the whip on your naked behind."

"Oh! Oh dear!"

"For spitting, twice as many, half to be inflicted on your naked bottom, the other half on the fronts of your thighs. You may prepare yourself, Marion, and I shall keep exact count, because this being your first whipping, I very much doubt your ability to retain an accurate accounting."

I pushed her lovely cascading black hair to one side so that I could grip her neck firmly with my left hand and, standing off to the left and with the whip in my right, raised it slowly so that she could not help but see it in the mirror in front of her. She uttered a sob, closed her eyes, and tensed herself with all her might. The lovely play of her muscles under the rippling satiny olive skin was enchantment itself. My cock was as hard as it had been at the very start of our afternoon in the Snuggery. But now there was a difference. Now I had learned much of Marion's secret nature, and now I could proceed undaunted to adapt and to shape it as Pygmalion fashioned his immortal Galatea, to my very own whims and fancies and lusts!

Chapter 9

I kept Marion waiting a long, languishing moment with my whip upraised and my left hand gripping the back of her slim neck. I must say that she showed now more bravery than could have been expected after her emotional breakdown and her confessional. I daresay if I had been thoroughly pacific with my intentions, I could have shown a nobility of character by forgiving her and releasing her and then cozening her into making love with me. But I think I correctly estimated that this would be a show of weakness on my part in turn and that she might try to regain her lost terrain and be haughtier than ever with me. No, I must harden my heart—just as my cock was hardened!—and proceed to a thorough subjugation of my beautiful sister-in-law to be.

At last I brought the whip down rather smartly across the top of her hips. It made a soft smacking sound, but it left no mark, although Marion sucked in her breath and nervously jerked, perhaps more from the torturing suspense than from the first stripe itself. "That is one," I counted aloud. She bent her head, closed her eyes, while I stared over her shoulder at the mirror, feasting my vision to the utmost. You cannot have any idea how really mouthwateringly tasty Alice's sister was, standing there stark naked except for her black stockings and the flouncy rosette garters, her legs slightly spread apart, her arms drawn up so high that her pectoral muscles were in fine bold relief, and the uptilting insolent pears of her bubbies surged out with a really dazzling elegance as if she would not be ashamed to enter them in a contest of love goddesses—including glorious Venus herself! Indeed, she would not have come off too badly in such a contest, in my private opinion.

I dealt the second cut a little lower down, just over the tops of her prominent firm bottomovals, and I enjoyed the sight of the lash clinging across those tensing hemispheres and the tip flicking round towards her tender groin. Marion gasped a little more loudly this time, nervously tried to shift from foot to foot, and dragged on her wrists. From the way her sides were trembling, and I could see the lovely ribcage plainly outlined against her taut warm olive skin, I knew that she must really be fatigued from the long duration of her atonement. But as this would join in the overall stress upon her nerves and her psyche to bring me the most delicious nuances of voluptuous gratification, I again hardened my heart and directed the third cut about an inch below the place where the second lash had kissed.

Her hips gave an involuntary swerve to this side, and to that; her head tilted back a little and her eyes opened. Intently following the reflection of her features—as well as her body to be sure!—in the huge mirror in front of her, I perceived that they were full of tears and that her nostrils were beginning again to dilate rather rapidly.

I did not keep her waiting for the fourth cut, but applied it almost instantly thereafter, yet exactly over the last place attacked. A reiterative stroke on bare flesh which has already been sensitized produces much more than a double effect of irksome heat, which radiates throughout the entire feminine nervous system and thus

112

aggrandizes the suffering—and also, the voluptuous tit-illations which a whipping always produces in a female of any sensitivity whatsoever, as any connoisseur of flag-ellation can tell you from experience.

The fifth lash took a little longer, and Marion nervous-ly glanced back for a second, then again bowed her head and stiffened herself. It cut directly across the plumpest curves of both naked hindquarters, producing a faint sob of "Aahh!" and a convulsive squirming which I found maddenly stimulating to my roused and now again sav-agely excited cock.

I made her wait almost a minute for the sixth lash, which wrapped the soft-substanced whip around the base of that mouthwateringly contoured backside of hers and possibly may have darted the tip of the lash in to-ward her furry gap, for she lunged to the left, sticking her bottom practically back at my swollen prick, while with a plaintive groan she entreated, "Ohh, please, please, s-sir, it hurts, it hurts!"

"To be sure it does, Marion, and it is meant to. What will it be, I wonder, when you receive your final eight strokes across the fronts of your thighs? You may ponder on that question while I complete the first portion of your whipping," I said. I now applied the two final cuts of that first sentence of eight lashes for the slap, placing them straight across, once more, the jounciest region of the summits of her naked olive-satiny behind. She groaned and sobbed a little, twisted and jerked, but in the main I had to admit that she had borne her eight strokes with relatively good grace, far better than a naughty teen-ager would have done if bent over a desk to receive chastisement for poor lessons or inattentive-ness or rudeness to her mistress.

But now I had an ingenious interlude to accord her which I knew would further surprise her tender flesh, unused as it certainly must have been during her three years of marriage to such imaginative treatments. Placing the whip on a tabouret to my right and behind her, I now took up the globe-box, opened and took out the longest, softest feather of the dozen, then closed the box and put it down beside the ship. During this pause, Marion again lifted her head and opened her eyes and stared into the mirror, doubtless to determine what I next intended. Her eyes widened a bit when she saw the feather in my hand, and then she blushed vividly and again closed her eyes and bowed her head, while a long tremor passed through that bewitching supple body of hers tethered by the silken ropes at her ankles and by the rope-pulleys at her updrawn wrists.

I squatted, and after a moment's study of her lovely quivering bare bottom and the beautiful merger of those long supple thighs sheathed so provocatively in the tightly moulding black silk hose, I extended the feather in my right hand and began to graze her sleek calves, then her kneehollows, and then on upwards along her thighs till I had reached the tops of the fine hose and was titillating the bare olive skin itself. Marion fidgeted throughout this unexpected treatment, and glanced back once or twice at me, and I also noticed that her thighs made involuntary jerks as if to clench together which, of course, the ropes at her ankles utterly prevented. I stroked her naked thighs a long moment, next artfully passed the side of the feather over the swelling curve at the base of her left buttock, then moved it to the other cheek at the same place, lulling her by this stroking and caressing but at the same time making her all too conscious of her nakedness before me and of all that she exposed so vulnerably to my slightest whim. Suddenly I passed the tip of the feather into the shadowy groove which separated her tensing naked bottomcheeks, and with the very tip of the plume tickled the secretive niche of her arse-hole. I made no attempt to open the cheeks of her behind to locate it definitely, but I knew that I had attained it from the sudden horrified little squeal of "Aahhh, oh, good Lord, what are you doing to me now, s-s-sir?" and her immediate violent contraction of all her bottom muscles to defend that most sensitive and most shameful of orifices.

Quite satisfied with her reaction, I resumed my little game, grazing the feather all over the quivering cheeks of her bare bottom, especially where the springy lash had inflicted its warm kisses on her choice firm satiny olive-tinted flesh. Her head tilted back again, and her breasts began to rise and fall with an erratic cadence, while long rippling tremors surged up and down her shapely long thighs. Yes, in many ways, Marion surpassed dear Alice in the complexity and deeply rooted latency of her feminine and sexual nature! What a treasure I had found in this blackhaired beauty who had come to score me off but who was now herself in the process of being scored!

I covered her entire bottom with those feathery caresses, ending at the chinkbone with its pronounced dimple, and Marion squirmed and wriggled salaciously at this last phase of the tickling, finally gasping, "Oh, for God's sake, s-s-sir, finish my punishment, I can't stand much more of this!"

"I am afraid you will just have to stand it, Marion, for as long as it pleases me. And I would not advise you to be insubordinate or surly at this stage, considering how nicely you are fixed for whipping, as I can readily add to your sentence."

With this, I moved round to face her, and she gasped aloud: "Ohh!" and her eyes were huge and glazed with her tears, for she beheld the furious erection of my prick, jiggling audaciously between my sinewy thighs as I

115

stood with the feather in my right hand and my left hand moving out to cup one of her beautiful bubbies and to squeeze and lovingly fondle it. As I did this, I began to tickle the nipple of the other globe, and Marion sucked in her breath and twisted her face away, groaning, "Oh don't make sport of me, you shame me so, it is disgraceful to take such advantage of a helpless woman!"

"If your husband had taken such advantage of you, I do not believe that you would be here this afternoon," I retorted as I continued to titillate the rosy bud of her nipple till I could see it quiver and tingle and stiffen with tumescence. Her face was absolutely flaming again, and her eyes were closed but her lashes could not help a restless nervous fluttering, nor could she control the rapid flaring and shrinking of her delicate nostrils. I playfully paraded the feather down her belly and spent a moment or two tickling the sweet niche in that deliciously smooth basin which would surely cushion a man mounted astride her in the very joust of love. The time had not yet come to tickle her cunt, but I certainly intended to do this without too much further delay. For it was time for the second part of her flogging.

With Alice, my readers may recall, I had induced the slightest dosage of cantharides into a glass of wine which I had given her before I had taken the maidenhead of her bottom. Now this was because she was such a pure virgin intact; but as Marion was not, I determined to guide her along the path of lust myself, relying not only on my own ability and vigor, but also on her own unleashed feminine powers—for unleashed they would surely be by the time I had finished with what I had in store for her.

I went behind her again, replaced the feather in the globe-box and took up the whip again. This time, without any warning, I drew back my arm and dealt her a cut right across the fleshiest part of her backside, but in a diagonal way, from right to left and giving the whip the slightest possible flick of my wrist as I concluded the stroke. This sent the tip whisking round the top of her hip and on towards the tender sloping basin of the groin and the lower abdomen, and she uttered a wild cry: "Aaarrr! Oh, don't, it hurts, oh how it hurts me! Oh do let me off now, sir, please dô!"

"Nonsense," I heartily rejoined, "You shall have seven more cuts just like that one on your naked bottom Marion, and then I am going to make you count off the final eight strokes across the front of your bare thighs. You are not even marked from your punishment thus far, so you need not try to deafen my ears with your entreaties for mercy. You are paying off your debt, which you have already agreed is grievous. Prepare yourself!"

With this, and with a backhanded stroke from left to right, I cut across her bottom to form a kind of X. Only the faintest pink mark showed on the warm olive skin of her backside, but the burning sting and especially where the lash crisscrossed its predecessor, caused her to lunge forward with a piercing shriek and to turn her face back over her right shoulder to appeal to me with hugely dilated, tearfilled eyes: "Ahhh! Oh my Lord, I can't bear such pain, oh, how it hurts my poor flesh! Do have mercy, I repent the things I did to you, sir!"

"For a woman of your maturity and marital experience, Marion, you disappoint me with your lack of originality," I taunted as I slowly raised the whip again to let her see what awaited her. "Why, a minx of twelve, up to be thrashed by the headmistress in a boarding school would have more ingenuity in trying to beg herself off. The most wicked sinner is always ready to repent when the lash begins to fall. No, Marion, it is only after you've

117

had your punishment that I shall treat with you as to your future behaviour towards me."

With this, I gave her the third cut, but this a horizontal slash from right to left just over the upper summits of her huddling, jerking, squirming bare bottomcheeks. Now I was using the full force of my arm, but I knew that the substance of this ingenuously fabricated whip would not break the skin and would hardly mark it for all my vigor. But it was thrilling to the extreme to watch the difference between the first part of Marion's whipping and this second portion, for now she cried out at every cut, in genuine anguish; and the way her body plunged and jerked and twisted, her hips jiggling and contracting and weaving, made me almost afraid that my cock would explode with admiration long before it had a chance to pay that ardent tribute deep within her cunt or arse-hole, depending where my burning needs might lead me.

I paused a little while to let her regain her strength as well as her voice; and as she twisted and squirmed, sobbing and tearful, I patted her tensing bottom with the whip and told her to get ready for the final strokes upon its sensitive terrain.

Next I gave her a very severe cut which made the whip cling across the base of both nether globes while the tip darted round to sting her tender inner thigh perilously near her furry cunt as I could well see in the mirror ahead of her. This lash produced the most piercing cry yet of the whipping, and a sudden furious tugging at her bound wrists as well as a hastily sobbed-out appeal for pardon. But I was deaf to all this. Now my eyes alone savored the joys she was providing me so unwillingly.

I made her wait for the last few strokes, but she had no reason to complain of their vigor when they finally attacked her tender oval-cheeked bare bottom. Each time the little whip visited the plump jouncy summits of her seat, Marion yelled out wildly and jutted herself forward in a kind of semi-arc like a bow, thus projecting out the furry nook of her cunt to the mirror in the most shameless way imaginable.

Seeing that she was rapidly losing her aplomb and courage which she had so admirably sustained through the first portion of her punishment, I decided to speed my own tempo in the hope that it would produce an even more complete annihilation of her will. I therefore moved round to face her, whip in hand, and I told her cruelly, "Now you are going to count aloud eight cuts across the tops of your bare thighs, enunciating each in a clear, loud voice so that there will be no mistake. For each cut that you do not count, you shall have an extra. Do you follow me?"

And before she could stiffle her sobs and groans and make any kind of affirmation, I drew back my right hand and slashed the little whip against the top of her left thigh, so that the lash wrapped round the lovely lithe column just below the groin.

"Arrrhhh! Ohh, no more, oh please stop, oh I can't stand it there, I can't, sir, do forgive me and let me off now!" Marion wailed as she lunged and twisted from side to side, dragging on her bonds above her head.

I waited a moment, and then I applied another cut over the very same place, wrapping the thong entirely around the lovely column which jerked madly under the stinging bite. A prolonged scream of anguish tore from Marion's gaping mouth as she twisted and jerked, but pitilessly I moved over to my left and sent the whip around the top of her right thigh this time as viciously.

"Eeeeowwll Oh my Lord, oh you are killing me—three, oh—three, oh end it, I cannot bear such suffering!"

"But it can hardly be three when you have not yet counted one, Marion," I told her, "It will go on being one until I hear you say so." And with this I applied a new slash which coiled the wicked little whip like a serpent hungrily clinging round her left thigh.

"Aiiii! Ohh, don't, I'll do whatever you want, I swear I will, sir, only for God's sake don't hit me on my legs again, please don't!"

I lowered the whip, trembling with the keenest kind of anticipation, and the veins along the shaft of my bulging prick were dark and gnarled with triumph lust. At last I had compelled haughty, arrogant Marion to offer herself of her own free will to escape from merited punishment. But I was not yet sure of what I wished of her, so I decided to test her compliance. "You mean that if I suspend the remaining lashes, Marion, you will agree without struggle or resistance, insult or injury, to do exactly as I order?" I demanded.

And, just to make certain that she understood my own obduracy in the matter, I doubled the little whip in my hand and shoved it right up against the mossy gape of her furry cunt, staring sternly into her tear-blurred eyes.

She shuddered violently, glancing down, then shrinking and squirming as she tried to remove that most vulnerable part of her delicious anatomy from the menace of the lash, and she huskily and sobbingly panted, "Oh, my God, yes, I can't stand this anymore, I really can't! Do what you want with me, and let me go!"

And thus, dear reader, my long-desired goal, that of the conquest of Alice's sister, was very nearly within sight!

Chapter *10*

Now that I had skillfully led this beautiful black-haired virago from a state of inimical warfare to imploring surrender, I proposed to teach her that which her husband had utterly failed in attempting, namely, the achievement of complete voluptuous bliss in the gentle art of mutual fucking. This logically was the only way I could thoroughly convert my intended sister-in-law if I did not wish her at some future time to think back in retrospect and entertain malicious and spiteful recollections of the afternoon, which might even lead her to commit audacious folly. Yes, if I could tap the hidden reservoirs of her female emotions, spin out all the latent, pent-up feverish urgencies in her luscious flesh to such a point that she no longer had control or prudery in her reactions, then I should have made her as ardent a love-slave as her beloved sister had now become.

So, although I longed to lie with her upon the luxurious couch and to take my fill of kisses and caresses and demand the same from her once I had wakened her to passion, I had again to steel myself in not granting her any respite from her by now quite uncomfortable poses and bondage.

I went behind her to take up the globe-box again and returned with it to my chair, seating myself directly in front of her. She gave a little cry and looked down at me, blinking her tear-filled eyes as she stammered, "Oh, what are you going to do to me now? Won't you have pity on me and let me go? My limbs ache everywhere, and it burns where you w—whipped me so awfully!"

"Presently, Marion, presently," I told her. Opening the glove-box, I choose the two very longest feathers and then put the box onto the floor at one side of my chair. With a feather in each hand, I leaned forward, seated on the edge, so that I could command the full expanse of her legs and middle as well as reach up without too much strenuous exertion to attack the panting turrets of her delicious bubbies.

I advanced the feather in my left hand towards her navel, flicking all around into that delightful nook, and then with my right hand swept the plume at the socket of her svelte, quivering left hip, tickling the shivering skin with a lingering peroration. She gasped and wriggled, bit her lips, and then closed her eyes, apparently resolved to show me with her stoicism that she was truly repentant and submissive. Now the feather in my left hand glided down her stockinged thigh, and stroked the fine black silk sheath about the knee up to where that lovely column joined her hip, while the feather in my right hand began to brush against her lower abdomen where the first black curls of her pubis flourished. As I lowered the tip of this feather toward the top of her cunt, Marion uttered a low sobbing groan and hoarsely stammered, "Oh, s-sir, I can't resist you any longer, I'm so exhausted and I hurt so, I'm ready to grant you whatever you wish if you'll only let me go!"

"Be patient, my gentle dove," I mockingly retorted, "for what I am doing will guarantee your newly found desire to show me kindness!" And with this, I lowered the feather in my right hand down toward the very top of her cunt and began to tickle her. Marion's eyes widened as she stared down at herself, and all of a sudden a fiery blush suffused her contorted, flushed tear-stained cheeks. Then she gnawed her lower lip and stiffened herself, but she could not help a sporadic trembling which shook her body from head to foot. I stared greedily at the thick verdure of that black crisp silky growth which so luxuriantly and protectively fleeced her slit. And I prodded the feather till the tip probed through the curls and touched the tip of her outer labia, then began very deftly to rasp it up and down the lip nearest me so as to sensitize it. Meanwhile the other feather continued its gliding touches all along her trembling thigh, now visiting the back of her leg with long and deliberate caresses. A tiny whimpering gasp escaped the naked victim as she tried to flex her muscles and renew their intrepid resistance to my blandishments.

Now the feather in my right hand moved over to the top of the other fleshy outer lip which helped to form that lovely fig, that sweet conch-shell which was her voluptuous cunt, and I proceeded to tickle it the same way. But now I glided the feather down to the very base of her slit and then back up again along that crinkly, fleshy pink lovelet, while the other feather now moved to the inside of her right thigh very near the furry gape which I was so intently beleaguering.

"Ohh, Oh what are you doing, oh my Lord, please stop —oh, I can't stand this—truly I can't—oh, sire, sire, be merciful, I'm only a helpless woman—ahh—ooohh—oh, no more, no more, in the name of mercy!" Marion panted as she began to jerk and twist, trying to wriggle her hips from side to side to disengage those feathers from their stealthy and relentless attack.

Now, slyly, I moved the feather in my left hand over to her cunt and in a trice had the soft downy tips of both of them moving up and down the two fleshy portals which concealed the road to paradise. Marion uttered a shriek and lunged her bottom backwards to escape this dual siege of her most sensitive and sancrosanct region. But all I had to do was pull my chair up an inch or so forward, and continue my ministrations. The ropes at her ankles as well as those dragging up her arms confined her to an extremely limited range of movement, just enough to excite me with her convulsive gyrations and her buckings and lungings which made her thighs and bubbies jounce and jiggle and express the luscious resilience of her naked flesh. And once again both feathers directed their diabolically persuasive caresses up and down the outer labia of Marion's twitching cunt.

"Aah—oh my G—God in heaven, oh, you'll drive me crazy, oh please, sir, oh, in the name of heavenly mercy I beseech you don't—oh do stop—eeeowww—oh, Lord, oh, it's too much, I can't bear it any longer, oh do have mercy on a poor helpless woman and spare me, sir!" Her vibrant voice was choked with sobs and gasps and groans as she twisted and arched and wriggled back and forth, her eyes now fixedly staring down at the two white plumes aimed at her crotch and whose tips were slyly tickling the quivering coral petals of her love-slit.

I drew them away so that I could have a look at the threshold of my coming attunement. Yes, definitely, the curly thicket of Marion's pussy-hair was ruffled and here and there I could perceive the exquisite crinkly surfaces of that voluptuous mucous membrane which was her temple of Venus, her nymph's grotto of satyr's delight. And then, with a cool little smile as I stared up at her, I thrust the tips of both feathers deep into her cunt and worked them back and forth!

The effect was magical! Marion emitted a wild, piercing shout of "Aaaah, Ohh, *nooooooo!!!* "And madly jerked her bottom backwards to draw herself away from the twin torments. But I followed, rapt with excitement, my prick throbbing with a ferocious urgency that told me I must not overestimate my powers of self-control in the face of such bewitching naked loveliness and enervation as my charming mature naked captive now evinced in my presence.

Once again the feathers dug into her quaking slit as far as I could shove them, then drew slowly out. Marion's head rose and fell, turned from side to side, her eyes rolling and brimming with great tears which broke and rolled down her contorted and flushed cheeks, and her trembling lips exuded whimperings sobs and moans, while her glorious bubbies heaved with furious turbulence. The spasmodic flexions which visited her straining, slightly gaping thighs demonstrated that she had reached a state of feverish approach toward the very voluptuousness which I meant to unleash.

I laid the feathers down on the arm of my chair and then I knelt down before her, as an acolyte might to his high priestess. I gripped the backs of her stockinged thighs and I put my tongue to the warm twitching and palpitating olive skin of her left thigh just above the rosette. How warm and tasty it was to savor! Not only was the subtle perfume with which she had evidently sprayed herself before her visit, but the stronger and more exciting compound of perspiration and the tang of her woman-smell coming from her delicious Venus-vent.

"Oh, don't do that for God's sake!" Marion fairly shrieked, as she dashed her bottom backwards as far as her pinions would permit. But my fingers rose up to grip the base of those olive-sheened nether ovals, and I forced her back to me and my tongue rasped upwards till it attained the sensitive, soft twitching flesh of the groin as I made my way towards the sweet fig of her voluptuous cunt.

"Nooooo!!! Oh my God, don't do that to me! Oh, I won't, I won't let you—oh, it's shameful—please stop, Oh, sir, oh my God, don't do it!" Marion wailed. I did not deign to answer. For now I pressed my lips full against the furry mound and I applied a loud smacking kiss on Marion's exquisite slit!

Her head fell back, her eyes lifting to the ceiling as if appealing to supernatural powers to save her from my onslaught. The perfume of her loins was like a potent aphrodisiac in my own excited system. And now, thrusting out the tip of my tongue, I rasped through the fleece until I came into contact with the palpitating prism of her cunny, until I felt the fleshy outer lip of her love-hole in helpless contact with my ardent and expert tongue!

Another wild yell burst from her throat as she desperately tried to clench her thighs, but all she did was to arch and squirm herself further against me, so that my tongue could furrow this way and that, making the sweet circle of that plump fig of hers, and the violent shudders that ran up and down her tethered body only added to my rising erotic fury.

Now I thrust my tongue as far as I could, deep into her cunt, finding the inner lips and prying between their constrained vigilance. Marion acted like one possessed, jerking her hips, sobbing and brokenly pleading with me not to shame her thus, tugging at her wrist-ropes, raising and lowering her head, her body shaken with constant tremors.

And at last I found the dainty clitoris, that nucleus of all her life, that harbinger of all her innermost yearnings and womanly passions. And my tongue dug at it and flicked at it and rubbed it back and forth till the convulsive jerkings of her hips and belly indicated that she was instinctively responding to my artful gamahuching!

"Ohh! Aahh, Oh dear God—oh no, oh please, sir, mer-

126

cy—you're killing me—I can't bear it, truly I can't, oh I can't, I can't! Do stop—oh I am going to faint, I am going to die—aahh—ooohhouuuu!!!"

The tearful, husky, almost incoherent tone of her voice was in itself a powerful stimulant to my desires. So, too, was the magnificent mobility of her naked bottom which my fingers so lustfully gripped, for I could feel the frantic contractions of her sphincter muscles as she tried to clench herself and to close that beleaguered vent which I was so salaciously saluting.

Now, finding the throbbing little button of her clitoris with my eager lips, I sucked at it and nibbled at it, and she fairly went mad with wrigglings and lungings, her shrieks clamorous as she implored me to desist. And then the glorious miracle of conquest—with a wild scream "Ahrrrr—oh, I'm dying—oh, you've killed me, *ooohhouuuu!!!*", Marion arched herself against me grinding her cunt wildly against my mouth and nose, as if she frantically sought the very caresses which she was announcing as being so hatefully odious to her, and then I felt the earthquake shatter her besieged naked body . . . and I felt at once the sticky sweet flow of her love-juices as I sucked her stiffening clitoris to the point of hot, abandoned come!

Chapter 11

I had at last proved that Marion was not nearly so frigid as she would have wanted me to believe, and at the same time I had also been roused to the most ferocious desire, as the aching pangs in my swollen prick insistently informed me. I went to the wall and touched the button, lowering the ropes that tractioned Marion's beautiful arms above her head, and she slumped, moaning softly in the aftermath of her furious climax. Squatting, I untied the knots around her slim ankles and then, quickly unsnapped the swivel-hooks of the pulleys and deftly lifted her up in my arms, my right arm under her stockinged calves, my left arm around her bare shoulders, and strode to the padded couch. I stared hungrily down at her panting bubbies and the stickied muff between her long, quivering thighs, signs of the fulfillment which my feathering and gamahuching had brought her. And now I was in the driver's seat, so to speak, for I had not brutally raped her, nor could she claim such indignity. No, aloof and imperious Marion had to admit her own female weakness in this just-concluded bout of nervous excitement. For if she had been frigid, she would never have achieved the shuddering spend to which I had compelled her. And thus her attitude toward me was bound to have significant alteration, which could only be in my own favor.

129

As I carried her towards the couch, she slowly opened her eyes and stared at me, then her face turned a vivid scarlet, and she immediately closed her eyes again, with a faint "Ohh!

"I have freed you, as you entreated, my lovely sister-in-law to be," I told her, "and now I shall take you at your word, that you will no longer resist my desires. Does your whipping still hurt you?"

"A—a little—Ohh, what must you think of me—I'm so ashamed to be like this, I can't bear to look at you, sir," she faltered, turning her face away from me and closing her eyes. I have no doubt that the spectacle of seeing herself carried naked in only her stockings and shoes in the arms of a totally naked man who had first fucked her and then gamahuched her was a really shattering blow to her cool poise and her affectatious haughtiness. And I was most curious, as you may well imagine, to know to what ends her new psychologically induced awareness of me would lead her.

I laid her down gently on the couch, telling her that I would bring her a glass of wine, but as I rose to leave her, Marion stammered, "Mayn't I go to the W.C. a moment, please?"

To hear that once vibrantly timbered voice take on so plaintive and child-like a tone to ask such a question almost made me laugh, but I maintained a straight face and told her that of course she might have a few moments to freshen herself, adding with just a hint of malicious irony, so as to show her that I was still lord and master in the Snuggery, "When you return, Marion, leave off your shoes. You have no idea how charming you are in just those stockings and rosettes."

At this she uttered another gasp, glancing down at herself as if for the first time, and the vivid color in her cheeks was evidence that she had lost completely the bold and insolent assurance she had brought with her at the outset of her visit to my apartment. As for myself, I settled myself in a chair near the couch and watched her walk to the bidet, observing how the magnificent spacious cheeks of her olive-sheened behind undulated and shifted with her rather hesitant tread.

For a moment I sat in rapt contemplation of the rosy future I had just assured myself. Yes, why not enter upon the sea of holy matrimony with delicious Alice, I asked myself. Certainly she was as tasty a morsel in bed as could be found, and in our era, when the hypocritical double standard of the male forbade the female to evince the slightest interest in sexual matters or to show—an even more heinous sin—the least ardor in conjugal relations, I surely could find no more amiable wife than sweet Alice who was already my passionate, willing and submissive lover.

And now that I had this hold on her beautiful sister, I felt that I could summon Marion to my bed when I wished, to entertain her with my favours, and make my wife-to-be, Alice, as enthusiastic and conspiratorial an aide in subjugating Marion to my bed-urges as could be wished for. No, marriage would not ordain the slightest cessation of my activities; on the contrary, because of the *menage* I would have from the outset, it would be practically as uninhibited a life as could be lived in a Moorish harem. These delightful thoughts occupied me until Marion emerged, her head bowed and not daring to look at me and—Oh, naive creature that a woman is, no matter what her age!—with one hand clasped shieldingly over the thatch of her cunt. She moved towards me, then stopped, obviously hesitant and suddenly shy, because now she was not acting under duress or the coercion of the bonds and fetters.

"Rest a bit, my dear," I told her gently, "while I bring you a glass of wine. I am in need of one myself."

Mayn't I—I put on a robe or something over me, sir?" she hesitantly murmured, still not daring to look up at me. "To be like this before you is—is so shameful . . . I—I feel like a fallen woman."

"But I prefer you this way, Marion, exactly because you are a woman now, and perhaps for the first time in your life," was my answer as I rose to fill the wine glasses and, again, very surreptitiously, drop in another tiny does of cantharides into hers. For now was definitely not the time for her to retrench from the passionate plateau to which I had so ingeniously brought her. She must not be allowed to go back to her once vaunted and arid realm of imperviousness. I came back to the couch on which she had seated herself, her thighs tightly clenched and with her hand still pressed tightly over her mossy groove. I handed her the glass and then clinked mine against it as I said cheerfully, "To our better understanding of each other, Marion, and to an ending of hostilities."

I took a hearty sip of my wine, watching her intently all the while. Finally, with a certain sigh which appeared to be that of resignation, she lifted her glass to her quivering lips and sipped daintily at it.

"Come now, I mean it," I urged. "We were enemies once, so let us be friends now, for it unthinkable that after what has occurred between us, you should still wish to be at my throat. Confess it now, Marion, did you not deserve your punishment?"

She shivered, and those beautiful bubbies of hers swiftly rose and fell, while the telltale crimson once more deeply colored her cheeks, as she at last whispered, "Is—is this the way you h-had my sister?"

"I will forget you have asked such an audacious question, my dear," I chuckled "I am not the kind of man who boasts over his conquests or scabrously dwells on the details. It could only be offensive to another woman. Do you then forget Alice, for she is away from the city and you are here beside me. It is to you I pay my admiration for your beauty. Are we friends now?"

"You—you must give me a little time to gather my senses about me," she petitioned in a low, sweet voice, while she continued to blush and avert her eyes from me. "It—it is like a terrible dream that I cannot believe I have dreamed . . . to find myself like this, so shamelessly unclothed, beside you whom I so detested."

"And do you still?" I pursued as I moved closer to her. "Finish your wine before you answer."

She did so, and I took the glass from her and set it down on the little tabouret near the couch, along with my own empty glass, and put my arm around her waist. She shivered violently and tried to move a little away from me.

"Do you still?" I repeated.

"I—I don't know what to think, either of myself or of you, sir," was her faltered answer.

"But you will admit that, just now, what I did to you was not so displeasing and that you did experience some pleasure from it?"

"Oh, please, I dare not think of such things . . . I am your prisoner and your victim, I am helpless and I cannot resist you longer, I know. Please, sir, do not shame me further by talking to me this way, I beg of you!" the blackhaired young woman stammered.

"Very well, then we shall not talk, for I am disposed to action. Look down there," I ordered as I took one of her slim hands and drew it toward my sinewy thigh. She gasped and blinked her eyes, shrinking a back a little, for she had just gazed upon my boldly swollen prick.

"It is you who have put me into this state, Marion, and it is you who must now alleviate my pangs," I added smilingly.

"Oh, will you not be content with what you have had from me now? Is that not a sign that I am contrite for what I did to you?" she implored.

I pondered a moment. Now I had compelled Alice under the lash to submit to bottomfucking, but I very much doubted I could bring Marion to voluntary submission to this demanding ritual. Possibly I could ultimately train her to frig me sweetly before the conclusion of this afternoon, but I also doubted that she would of her own accord salute my prick with her sweet lips and tongue. Of course, after the interlude with Lady Betty Bashe and her daughter Molly, Alice had sucked and tongued me, as had her lovely maid Fanny and the lovely young widow Connie. But to expect so salacious and intimate a procedure from the so-recently embattled brunette beside me during the course of a single afternoon—even granting I had already altered her concepts of fucking and loveplay to an incredible extent—would be much too greedy. I was content to pursue the rehabilitation of Marion at a leisurely gait, for only a greedy glutton seeks to eat up all the tidbits at a single repast. And the prospect of having more delightful games to play with her and things to teach her in the future was certainly an enticing one.

So, tightening my arm about her bare waist and moving until my naked thigh pressed firmly against hers, I whispered, "But if I were to let you go now, Marion, you would never really know my feelings toward you. You would not conceive their true sincerity. I wish you to believe this, for it is the truth. And as for yourself, you have not yet answered my question. Did you not, there at the last when I was kneeling before you, find greater pleasure than your husband had ever given you?"

"Oh, please—I don't dare speak of such a thing. Please be satisfied, sir, and don't press me."

"You must call me Jack now, for we are soon to be related by marriage," I chuckled, as I took one of her hands and held it in mine, my eyes feasting on the turbulent rise and fall of her splendid bubbies. "But I do insist on an answer, or I am very much afraid I shall have to treat you to another taste of the whip on your lovely bottom. And this time, Marion, I shall tie you down over that piano stool which will project the cheeks of your naughty behind upward in a most tight and inviting way, to make the whip bite much more cruelly than you felt it before."

"Oh, no—I couldn't bear any more. Please, no! Oh, J-Jack, how can you be so heartless toward me?" and she turned her beautiful dark blue eyes to me, filled with tears. She was absolutely devastating in this new penitent and submissively fearful mood!

"The fact of the matter is, my dear Marion," I replied, "that your marriage failed because you were mated to an incompetent oaf who did not realize what a sensitive, charming and utterly desirable girl you are." At this she shivered a little and stared wonderingly at me. Once again I had found a key to her personality: for all she referred to herself as "Alice's strict aunt," there could be no doubt that she was susceptible to flattery and that she had a vain streak in her makeup.

Pressing my advantage, therefore, I resumed: "That is undoubtedly why you were unhappy with him. That is also why, as moreover you yourself plainly intimated a little while ago, you had such a low opinion of me, and you lumped me with this intolerable and dullwitted boor. Now, you asked me just a moment ago what methods I had used to seduce your sister. Well, I will tell you this: she is now unshakeably my sweetheart because I knew how to plumb her emotional depths and to bring her to happiness which she did not realize was latent within her own lovely body. That can be done only by a man who has both appreciation and consideration for a woman whom he possesses. And I thus promise you that I believe I can change your contemptuous opinion of men if you will surrender yourself and let me take the initiative I know best how to take."

"You—you mean you want to h-have me again?" she whispered as her blushes deepened furiously this time.

"I do indeed. Was it so horrible then for you, just after your whipping?" again I demanded.

I felt her shivering against the circle of my left arm. She bowed her head and finally, after a long moment, slowly shook it.

"There, you see, Marion," I exulted, "because what I did was not out of selfishness at all, but solely to convince you that you were capable of the deepest and most loving emotions a passionate woman can have. And since I have thus allayed your fears of how a man can act when he has imagination, do you now submit yourself so that together we may both achieve pleasure from this afternoon's engagement."

"If—if only it wasn't so w-wanton, J-Jack," she quavered. "If it were at night and the lights out and we couldn't see each other—"

"But that would be to deny the feast of love which is provided as surely through the eyes as through the rest of our bodies, Marion," I smilingly explained. "And now, enough of talk. You have said you will submit yourself, and I now call upon you to redeem that pledge. You have my word that I will not hurt you if you so surrender."

136

Her little nod was again one of resignation, followed by a deep sigh of almost melancholic proportions. I rose, then gently cupped her panting bubbies and gently forced her down upon her back. The couch was amply wide and long, and as she lay cushioned there upon it, clad in only those black silk hose and the flouncy rosettes, I stood for an idyllic moment contemplating her delicious charms, while she put a hand over her face in the most charmingly childlike of gestures.

"Now, Marion, I am going to make love to you in such a way that when we come together, you will be eager for me as well as ready," I told her.

With this, I knelt down and, almost reverently cupping her right bubbie with both my hands, began to kiss it gently and slowly, covering the luscious pear-shaped globe with tender, grazing little kisses, but at first avoiding the aureole and nipple. Marion's free hand lay at her side, as she continued to cover her eyes with the other, and I glanced quickly down at her legs and noticed that her dainty toes were curling and twisting, a sign that she was torn between anxiety and enervation. The cantharides would be my ally now, I knew. Already her nipples were darker and more turgid than when I had first stripped her and reveled in the first view of her delectable nudity.

"Do you find this distressing?" I murmured, as I brushed my lips just over the dark coral lovebud.

"N-no. Ohh—ohh, n-no!" she breathed.

I now took the nipple between my lips and delicately sucked it. Marion uttered a strangled gasp and suddenly put her hand against my forehead, as if to shove me away, so I sternly commanded, "You are not to interfere or to forbid me anything now, on pain of a good sound whipping over the piano stool, my girl," and then I took

137

her nipple between my lips and this time slowly ran my tongue over the crinkly bud.

Marion squirmed on the couch, and now her hand resumed its place over her eyes, while she turned her head towards the back of the couch, so as to hide from me. Her free hand was now clenched, the nails dug into her dainty palm, as no doubt she tried to steel herself against all these new sensations which, although she had been a married woman for three years, she had never tasted until this very afternoon.

Continuing to cup her bubbie with my left hand, I now moved my right down over her belly, caressing it in a most soothing manner. Her thighs were still clenched, and nervous spasms made the muscles flex exquisitely under the warm, olive skin, quite visible through the fine gauge of her black silk stockings. As my right hand lowered down to the abdomen where her black silky love-hairs began to flourish, she uttered a gasp and again her free hand clutched at mine.

"Do that again," I told her," and over the stool you go, Marion, and you will have at least twenty cuts over your naked bottom, so be warned."

At this she drew her hand away as if she had touched a redhot stove, and now covered her face with both hands, shivering in a paroxysm of apprehension and nervous titillation. I thereupon resumed my sucking and tonguing of her swollen and darkened nipple, while I passed my right hand over the plump mound of her cunt, and I began to stroke the silky thick curls which veiled that amorous orifice.

I felt her thighs stiffen as she summoned all her muscles to her defense. My forefinger entered through the thicket and found the moist twitching outer labia of her cunt. "Ohh! Oh, please don't tickle me there! Please

138

don't, Jack," she moaned, and again she rushed a hand to grasp at my wrist.

"You know what I promised you, Marion," I said sternly. "I am going to tie you down over the stool very firmly and give you a whipping you won't forget for disobeying my orders."

"Oh, Jack, please—Oh, please don't! Please don't be cruel to me now. You've already whipped me so hard—please don't, Jack! It's all so new to me, Jack. Please be merciful to me and don't wh-whip me again," she pleaded brokenly.

"Then will you give me your solemn word not again to restrain me or to make me take my hand away while I am preparing you for love, Marion?" I demanded.

"Y—yes—ohh, I never dreamed a man could do such things to a woman—oh, hurry then, before I die of my shame," Marion groaned.

Thus given *carte blanche*, I nibbled at her swollen nipple for a bit, then let my right forefinger slip between the fleshy, moist outer lips of her slit to find her clitoris. The moment I touched it, she uttered a sobbing gasp of "Ohh, please, you mustn't tickle me there, you'll kill me, you'll drive me crazy touching me there! Oh Jack, if you've any feeling for me at all, don't do that!"

"It's because I do have feeling for you that I do what I do, so let's have no more complaints, my girl, or it will be over the stool with a vengeance," I warned.

All this while, dear reader, I could feel the rigidity of my prick savagely insisting upon alleviation, but fortunately I was able to master the urge because I knew what delicious bliss I could accomplish by purposeful prolongation with my beautiful, enervated captive.

My forefinger began to graze her clitoris this way and that, till finally with a sobbing groan, Marion lifted up her knees and dug her stockinged heels into the couch, flexing her muscles and wriggling her toes in a very dither of sensual awareness. Her head also began to move restlessly from side to side, and now she had removed her hands from her face and had them clenched just to the side of her panting bubbies. I moved forward to attack her left breast now, my lips at once attacking the perky bud, sucking and nibbling at it, while my tonguetip flicked at it repeatedly. Her low groans and sobbing little whimpering cries excited me enormously, and it was all I could do to remain deliberately calm so I could be the mentor and guide to Marion's first really cooperative fuck.

This new attack brought me into closer proximity with Marion's naked flesh, and she gasped again as my forefinger pressed her clitoris down into its secretive lair of pink, moist warm loveflesh. I heard her groan, "Ohh my Lord! Ohh!" and then her knees clamped and her bottom squirmed in an unmistakable rhythm of response. My finger and the cantharides had begun to waken her long-rejected passions to the kindling point; I had now ignited a fire in her womb which needs must be put out with the extinguishing jet of my virile spunk. But I wished that blaze to be so incendiary that it would consume her entirely and thus purge her forevermore of her affected aloofness.

My tongue rubbed against her throbbing nipple as I sucked and loudly kissed the sweet turgid bud. Now my left hand slipped under her shoulders, and our bodies thus conjoined. Her knees swung apart and her stockinged heels rubbed erratically back and forth over the surface of the couch as she became gradually overpowered by the myriad sensations teeming in her matrix. Yet deliberately I continued to frig her stiffened lovebutton, which would soon knell the doom of her prodigious chastity. For that chastity came out of denial of self as well as denial by the stupid selfishness of her former husband, and I had no pity on it because it would destroy her and sour and dry her up before her time. I meant her to burgeon as a true woman, perhaps more passionate even than lovely Alice had become.

Now I left her bubbies to glide my lips down her waist and to her belly, pausing lingeringly at her sweet navel, which I licked all around with the tip of my tongue, as she arched and squealed, "Aaahh! What are you doing to me, Jack? I can't stand all this—I'm going to faint, I know I am!"

Every time my finger pressed down her clitoris, her body jerked and arched and wriggled in the most fascinating way. And then—oh, miracle of conversion—I suddenly felt her arms grasp my neck, but not in hostility. Her fingers were trembling as they pressed against my flesh with a kind of pleading urge to go on with what I was doing. And thus Marion first gave me her womanly accolade which bestowed on me the right and the might to topple her citadels of prudery, pernicious chastity, and hypocritical frigidity!

I glanced at her as I continued to suck and nibble at her left bubbie-bud, the while my right forefinger continued its titillation of her turgid clitoris. Her eyes were wide and glassy now, and it was not entirely the effect of the cantharides which had brought this about. Her nostrils flared and shrank interminably, and her lips were parted and moist, her face turned slowly from side to side as if seeking restlessly some point of comfort, some fulcrum of repose which was denied her. But her lovely slim hands were clasped together just above her bosom and her fingers were twisting nervously in her stress. My chest pressed down upon her right bare bubbie, and I felt to my exultation the shuddering upheaval of that luscious globe, the rasping friction of her stiffened dark

141

coral nipple against my prickling skin. For a moment I left off tickling her lovebutton so that I might frig the inner lips of her cunt, and Marion moaned, "Ohh, Jack, Oh dear God, I can't stand it, I just can't, I'm going to faint I know I shall!"

"Are you ready to be had, then, my dear?" I hoarsely asked her, for I must admit that by now my own powers of control were waning fast.

"Oh yes, yes. Do what you want to me, before I go mad with all this torture," she gasped.

"Then you must ask me to fuck you, Marion," I replied. How I savored that graphic, colorful word which conjures up the mind all the salacious images of welded bodies, straining flesh, soft trembling lips and flaring nostrils, the sweet dig of agitated supple fingers under the tension of lustful frictional impalement!

"Jack, what are you making of me—what have you done to me—Ahh! Ohh! How it tickles, how it burns me there!" she panted as my forefinger now returned to frig her swollen love-button. Her knees rose further into the air, her stockinged heels digging restlessly at the couch, spurning it as once she had wished to spurn me in her vengeful and haughty mood. But now this spurning was of a different caliber, induced by the womanly pangs which now beset her vitals. Now she had been stripped to the moment of truth and it was approaching for her in the devastating and over-powering compulsion of all her carnal lusts! For assuredly she felt these, just as I, the male dominator, experienced the glory of my virile rut.

"I want to hear you say that, Marion, or I shall have recourse to the whip again," I warned. "Tell me you are ready to be fucked, my beauty. Ask me humbly and sweetly to fuck you, Marion!"

And with this, I gouged my forefinger between the

142

inner lips and on into her tight, warm sheath, exactly as I meant to do with my fulminating prick.

Her hips weaved and jerked about, then her knees flung out, only to clamp shut again as she arched up her pelvic basin to the inroads of my fingers. It was as if she had given up the struggle and was now yielding up her body to its own volition, its own greedy and hungry quest for satisfaction. No longer could stately, haughty Marion boast of the veneer which had protected her and at once blighted her married life. Now she was melted into wanton flesh and throbbing sinews and nerves and hot veins and pulsing membranes that burned with a single furious fire . . . the fire of uninhibited lust!

"Aahh—oh, Jack—Oh my Lord—yes, ooohhh—don't tickle me there any more, please—oh yes, f-fuck me instead, oh yes, please fuck me now!" at last my beautiful captive averred in a sobbing, husky voice!

I mounted onto the couch, lying on my left side towards her, slipping my left arm under her shoulders, and I pressed on her trembling lips the most passionate of kisses. Her lips opened under mine, and I delved my tongue in between them to take prompt and gracious advantage of her sweet, helpless invitation. A shudder seized her as my right hand boldly glided round her lip and under her firm juicy bottom, revelling in its warmth from the lashing and from the additional glow of her own smouldering womanly passions.

"Put your left arm around me, Marion,' I commanded, and was obeyed. "Now with your other hand feel for yourself to what a state you have brought my cock."

"Oh, I could never do that—don't make me do such a thing—oh, you wicked man to ask so much of a helpless woman! Aren't you satisfied with this? You have shamed and disgraced me, defeated me, and I have begged you to do that to me which I never thought I would want any

143

man to do again, after Harry—and still you are not satisfied?" she sobbed.

Now was the time for me to be harsh and relentless with my captive, if ever I wished to make her my love slave, and that was why I cynically retorted, "I can as easily strap you down on this couch with your bottom upturned to the whip if you continue to act like a spoiled and pampered child! Reach down your hand and take hold of my cock. You are going to guide it to your cunt, Marion. Yes, your cunt, my girl. Did your famous Harry ever use that word, Marion?"

"Ohh!" she gasped in an aghast tone, her eyes fixed on me in anguished appeal.

"What did he call it, then?" I asked, as I seized her hand and brought it down upon my stalwart prick.

"Oh, don't make me tell you—Oh, please take me, have me but don't shame me in this unendurable way, Jack!" Marion whimpered.

I forced her hand down upon my hard, rigid weapon. She tried to draw it away, but I held it in a vise of steel as I went on: "Grasp it. Feel it. Put your fingers over it, and learn its dimensions. Squeeze it gently. It will soon be inside of you, my girl, and you must know its measure and girth so as to prepare yourself for it."

Trembling, her slim long fingers gripped my bulging shaft and—oh what delicious pleasure was in that sweet touch of hers—doubtless the first time she had so held a man in all her life, even as wife and consort.

"I will not only use the whip on your bottom, I will use a feather in between the cheeks of that impertinent backside," I threatened. "Speak. Tell me how he described that place I have been tickling. At once!"

I felt her fingers convulsively clutch against my prong as she forced herself to utter in a dying voice, "My—my

144

p-pussy. Oh, Jack, now you know everything about me, you have all my dreadful secrets, and I am so ashamed!"

"Shame is exactly what turned you into a hateful jade, Marion," I declaimed. "From this moment on I shall change all that. And now prepare yourself for fucking, my beauty. Go ahead, pass your fingers all over my cock and balls. Discover for yourself what is going into that tight, eager cunt of yours—for I know it is eager now. You cannot deny any longer your own desires, for your flesh betrays you, Marion."

She put her hand over her eyes again, while with the other she docilely though hesitantly palpated my aching prong. I kissed her trembling lips and then the hollow at her throat, where I could feel the triphammer, pressing pulse in the feverish cadence of her life-rhythm. Her skin was moist and sweet, as never before, and her naked body writhed and squirmed on the couch, and now the cantharides were doing their work along with her first honest affirmation of her sensual yearnings.

"Now prepare yourself for the sacrifice, Marion," I told her. Then I mounted between her quivering stockinged legs, kneeling and lowering myself towards her, my prick bobbing like a cork on an angry sea as I commanded, "Take your hand and open up that sweet, inviting cunt of yours to welcome me!"

She groaned and turned her face to one side, but all the same, her sweet, trembling hand did as bidden. Oh wonder of delight, to watch this transformation in a virago who had become a passionate and submissive slave in so short a span!

Guiding my cock with my right hand, I approached it to the pink, twitching, moist apperture and let the broad head of my spear engage itself just inside the lobby of her exquisite cunt. Then, tightening my grip under her shoulders with my left arm, I slowly lowered myself. As

145

she felt my prick press between the inner lips of her citadel, Marion uttered a sobbing groan: "Oh, Jack! Oh my
Lord! Jack, Jack!" and then suddenly, miraculously, her
bare arms enfolded me as if to bring me down upon her.
Her eyes closed, her head flung back, her nostrils flaring
and shrinking wildly, my future sister-in-law to be thus
symbolically gave up the final vestige of her resistance
and welcomed the man she had sworn to defame and de-
grade and destroy!

I slowly felt myself sink to the very balls inside that
narrow sheath, and words cannot depict the thousand
and one raptures I felt in gouging along that heavenly
channel of Venus. My left hand passed under her bottom, to support as well as steer her, to inculcate in her
the meaning of the thousand subtle signs by which a
man informs his lover of his pace, his gait, his cadence in
the sweet art of fucking. Her fingertips pressed harshly
into my back, and this too was an additional joy to me.
For it was as if she had been reborn and was awaiting
tensely and vibrantly the moment of veracious passion to
which her beauty entitled her, to which her long-denied
ardent personality had shaped her, only to be warped by
the lusterless and selfish initiation of a doltish husband.

Slowly I drew myself back to the very brink of her
cunt, and a long gasp evinced her pleasure in this maneuver. My lips on hers, my tongue delving repeatedly
along the roof and the gums of her mouth, I savored her
sweet nectar, while my prick foraged with long slow digs
to the very ell-length of my weapon and then back to the
quaking portals that guarded the way into her mature
matrix.

"Am I hurting you now, Marion?" I demanded.

"Ohhh—ohh—Jack—n-no oh Lord—is this possible?
Oh, I am trembling all over, I am going to faint away—
it's unbearable—oh Jack—oh please—oh—oh—oh!"

Now both my hands slipped down to the velvety warm cheeks of her bottom and, gripping them solidly, I began to quicken my pace within her agitated, squirming cunt; with long skewering thrusts, I furrowed her, and her body began to jerk and twist and arch under my repeated prongings. Now, to my utter bliss, she was kissing me of her own accord, and her fingers were digging into my bare shoulders and gouging the skin in her agitated enervation, in her longing to meet me more than half way along the road of rut!

To feel her naked bubbies flatten against my heaving chest, to feel our bodies clash in a sweet conflict which was a thousand-fold distant from that conflict which she had promised me upon her visit, to feel best of all the clamping, tightening, constricting pressures of her vaginal wall against my embedding prick was to taste the most bounteous rapture of which man is capable on this ephermeral earth.

I ground my teeth to hold back my frenzied, bubbling spunk, so that I could bring her with me to that apex of amorous ecstasy. Now at each time my prick delved down to the hilt inside of her, Marion uttered a little whimpering sigh and clutched me all the tighter, and now her legs came into play as she wound her stockinged calves tightly against my sinewy legs and gave herself up totally to the abandonment of all her former prudery.

How her bottomcheeks clenched and flexed and jerked against my digging fingers! Her eyes were hugely dilated, glazed and unseeing as they stared into my looming face, and her mouth attacked mine now with a voracity which could not have been believed an hour or so ago.

I quickened the stabbing momentum of my thrusts, feeling myself almost upon the brink of explosive fury. I felt her bottom jerk and bound and arch as she met me,

147

plying me with her velvety flesh, digging herself against me to take every inch into her very depths.

And then suddenly, with a wild cry, Marion twisted her face to one side, her nails pitilessly digging into my armpits, and a loud shriek clamorously burst from her; I felt her body heave and buck against mine, as with a final savage fury, I drew myself back and thrust myself to the hilt and then felt my prick vibrate with the hot lashing vigor of my seed into her warm, tight sheath.

As she felt that hot gismic tribute burst against the tender flesh of her womb, Marion uttered another loud cry and pressed her lips to mine as she lifted herself to absorb all of me.

And then it was over, and she lay moaning and gasping, with me atop her, my limpening prick still burrowed in her quaking cunt. The moment of truth had come for Marion. She was beyond dissembling now; all her body vibrated and shook with the tempestuous elemental fury that had overpowered her and made her mine.

Chapter 12

I held Marion trembling and shuddering in my arms long after her first true spasm had passed. Her face was crimson, her nostrils uncontrollably flared and shrunk and the turbulent swelling of those beautiful bubbies showed unequivocally that this was perhaps the most sincere manifestation she had ever shown in the act of love, or so at least I could conjecture after what she had already disclosed concerning her frustrating marital experiences.

When I was certain she was quieted, I withdrew from her and hastened to my water closet to repair the wounds of the fray. I returned with a wet hand towel and knelt beside her and gallantly did her toilet for her, much to her sighing embarassment. To my great delight, she showed no inclination to move from her sprawled and completely abandoned pose on my couch, and the enhancement of her olive-warm nakedness against the cushions and the dark upholstery of my couch of love was a most pleasant vista for my eyes.

"Whatever has become of me?" she murmured in a low, faint voice, passing a hand in front of her eyes, and then she burst into convulsive tears and sobs. It was doubtless the reaction of being aware that despite all her prudery and haughtiness, she discovered she was simply mortal, after all, a discovery which had, as you may well imagine, entranced me to the utmost!

"But my dear Marion," I gallantly protested, "there is no need to feel such despondency with yourself. You have been for the past half hour the most amiable of consorts, and you have absorbed my attentions to the fullest. I could not have paid any other woman a more enthusiastic and passionate tribute than I have shown you, which should console you completely and force you to take a more sanguine view of yourself, at least as seen through my eyes."

"But I have been shameless . . . wicked and wanton . . . like the worst trollop on the streets who hires herself out to any man. Oh, what shame is mine, to have been so weak! If I had only had more courage, you could not have made me yield myself so lewdly!" she sobbed.

Now doubtless her reaction was also caused by the immortal maxim which, rendering from the Latin, holds that after love, every animal is sad. But I felt no such sadness; quite the contrary, I felt a geniality and zest for her companionship, for she had now entered into my sphere and was of considerable import to my future hopes and aspirations for pleasure. I would certainly be loath to relinquish so delicious a mistress, now that she had shown her true capacities for sucking. Oh, by no means was her education yet complete in this tender art, and she had not even touched upon some of its more secretive and exciting variants, such as the sweet bliss a woman of her beauty and proportions could give to a man by taking his prick into her softly beautiful warm lips and plying her tongue nimbly and delightfully upon it, or by using her fingers to frig her delicately and whet his virility to a supreme manifestation of his lust for her soft cunny. Nor had I even introduced her into bottom-fucking, a variant with which I had begun her sister's amorous training so memorably.

I took her hand and brought it to my lips and kissed it

as tenderly as any gallant at court, and I said to her soothingly, "My dear sister-in-law to be, be of good heart and cheerful disposition, for you have done away with your hateful past and with your embittered philosophy which held you back from realizing the joys of the honest and eager flesh. You have my promise, nay, my solemn word, that this will be a secret between us. But I tell you admiringly and in all honesty myself, that I hope this will not be the only time I shall be privileged to enjoy your lovely body. And particularly this tender and delicious grotto which has served my prick so ably just now."

And with this, putting my hands to her quivering hips, I bent my head and implanted on her mossy cunt and most prolonged and tender and adoring of kisses.

At once her hands clutched at my head, and in a sobbing, piteous tone, she implored, "Oh, Jack, how can you plunge the dagger deeper into my wounded heart, when you have left me so desolate and with so little respect for myself? I dare not show my face in your presence, or even in my sister's, for I shall know every time what has passed between us. I have given you more than ever I gave poor Harry, for all his faults, and the dreadful thing is, oh, that you have forced this from me, and I know that I am not your equal in cleverness or in cunning—but when you were having me just now, I very nearly swooned away and was no longer mistress of myself. For a moment I forgot the shame and the odium of being forced to obey your wicked passions."

"But think on it gently for a moment, dear Marion," I urged, as I retained my soothing and caressing hold of her sleek naked hips and kept my face but inches from that mossy groove which had done my cock such sweet service, willy-nilly. It was as if, indeed, I were addressing that portion of her which had suddenly become so vital to my pleasure. "If, as you have just said, my passions were truly wicked, then you yourself would not have shared them with me. For you were ardently moved, my beautiful Marion, as if you truly were in love with me, to see the tumult of your lovely breasts, to feel the tremoring of your voluptuous bottom, and best of all to feel the quaking surges of those secret walls along your temple of love as they besieged my onrushing prick, was to know that I was not selfish in letting you glimpse what divine bliss there can be in fucking!"

The use of this word, so violently terminating my flowery discourse, dear reader, was purposely intended, first to lull the beautiful Amazon into a flattered state wherein her vanity would be restored and she could preen herself much after the manner of a peacock that has momentarily had its glorious tail go unnoticed. Then, the lecherous word, the word that would evoke in her secret mind all the sweet naughtiness of what she had just done, even though she had tried to desperately to hold back her response to my priapic powers.

At any rate, my ruse partly succeeded, for she managed to lower her hand and to stare at me with wide and humid eyes, although at this moment she suddenly manoeuvered her other hand to cover that delightful Mount of Venus. And she stammered, "Is it really true, Jack, that you do not think me cheap or wanton? Is it possible that the two of us, such enemies at the beginning, could really have shared what loving husband and wife can know?"

"It is, it is indeed, my beautiful sister-in-law to be," I cried exultantly, "and if you will but let me try a final time before I release you from your sweet captivity, I will prove it. And I vow that I will never think you cheap, for that would be to think myself cheap too, and then I would not be a fitting mate for your dear sister whom I love, not only with all my heart . . . but with this too, dear Marion."

As I said "this too," I drew her fingers off her cunt and, moving slightly forward on my knees, forced them to clasp my thoroughly limpened but newly cleansed prick.

"Ohhh! Oh, I dare not—oh, Jack, oh, this is so new and dreadfully embarrassing, will you not spare me? Have I not paid my debt to you now many times over?"

"Yes, in all sincerity, I would be an ingrate and a dour wretch if I were to hold you to further payment of our score," I told her truthfully. "But now I ask you, since you have taken this first tremendous step toward taking me for what I am and not for what you thought I must be, can it not be done in honest endeavor and in token of friendship?"

"What—what must I do then, to show you that I do not any longer bear rancor against you, s-sir?" she tremulously quavered.

"Why, then," I told her jubilantly, for I knew her now to be upon the brink of total surrender and of renunciation of all previous enmity between us, "you can begin by seeing me as I am, just as I have seen you as you are, Marion. Frankness and honesty is a precept as highly regarded in fucking as in every walk of life and in every endeavor. Each part of your charming person is delicious, and cumulatively the total comprises the most entrancing lover. But you, in turn, must regard, the male instrument of your newly acquired pleasure, constituted as separately and then again as cumulative, by which I mean, do not shy from looking, nay, from touching that which you see perhaps in its rightful state perhaps for the first time. ust as this—" and here I lifted up her sweet hand which had sought to cover her lovely cunt and which I had brought to touch my prong, "is now a thousandfold more dear to me than when I did not know

153

your person save in the formidable prudery of your garments and judged you as dull of mind and clouded of spirit as you made your body seem by hiding it."

Oh, yes, I knew how specious was my argument with Marion, but remember I had brought her a considerable distance, and in so short a time as to make this alteration in her almost inconceivable. I confess I had not dreamed to have gone so far. Oh, there was no question that by my artful frigging and feathering and gamahuching I could bring about the vengeance I had always sought over her, but it was evident that I had mastered her, truly mastered her, and she startled me by participating in the battle so that it was not always so one-sided, and thereby she had gained both my respect and my newly kindled desire. Yes, I wished to fuck her again, but this time it would be in joy, not in enmity, and would be enjoyed on both sides. This, then, was the thread of my argument.

And I added, while she was wavering, her face once more scarlet, still staring at me, considering this revelation of male wisdom, "Was it because you were brought up to believe that to show one's body even to one's husband is sinful and wanton? Was it also because during your marriage to that inconsiderate brute, he never once undertook to explain to you the mysteries of Cythera and of Priapus, but sinfully and brutally took that which he believed to be his right, without considering your own fair estate in the matter?"

I saw her nod and close her eyes, then turn her face away. Her fingers tightened in mine, but I drew them forcibly again to my cock, which was beginning to show signs of new life, thanks to all this philosophical discussion whilst in the nude, and I confess that seeing her naked on the couch, clad only, in those delicious and naughty black hose with their provocative rosettes to

154

hold them firm and unwrinkled to her lovely legs was even more whetting to my lustful appetites than all the philosophy of heaven and hell combined.

"Then," I resumed, feeling her fingers shrink and nervously jerk as I continued to press them against the candid manifestation of my manhood so that she could not mistake it for what it was, "is it not true, by the same token, that as a woman of beauty and wit and spirit, you yourself have a right to expect tenderness and the sharing of mutual joys in lovemaking?"

Again she nodded, lowering her eyes and blushing hotly. We were at least well on the right track now, I knew. All her shibboleths and old-wives' tales which had made her frigidly disdainful towards this exquisite cohesion between man and maid were now being brought into the piercing and fierce light of discussion and debate, and I meant to purge her mind of them so that she would no longer be cluttered by unfounded distaste for the joyous sport of fucking.

"Well, then, in that event, my dear Marion," I murmured, "let us joyously as friends who have nothing to hide from each other, become acquainted with each other's capabilities and whims, and enter into a companionship which cannot but be wholesome for us both. Try to forget the pain I caused you, but if you do remember it, tell yourself that it was merited and that it led to this happy understanding between the two of us. Now, are you more inclined to view me as a friend than as an enemy?"

She had averted her face toward the back of the couch, but she did not try, I noticed, to pull her fingers away from my cock. They seemed to quiver as if half afraid and half eager to assay the knowledge she had so long shunned.

I moved closer to her on the couch now, and took her

in my arms. To my great delight she did not draw away, nor did she withdraw her hand from my soft cock, which by its new tremors under her soft touch once again warned me that its amorous energies were not yet exhausted. My left arm moved under her armpit and around, so that my hand might taste and cup and palpate the sweet, shuddering goblet of her bubbie, and I bent my head to kiss the nipple of that other sweet love-turret nearest me, whilst my right hand stroked the shivering, silk-sheathed contours of her lovely thighs.

Momentarily I pondered on the dilemma which might be mine should Alice discover that I had turned her strict and somewhat feared sister into a passionate accomplice, but, as you will see, dear reader, Marion herself solved this predicament most happily for me and all others concerned in my happy entourage of loving partners.

"What beautiful breasts you have, dear Marion," I murmured. "One might well spend an entire night praising and adoring them. And to each facet of your luscious form, another night might be entirely devoted. When I think that your oafish consort ignored such loveliness for so long, I sorrow for the stupidity of my own sex. But in my humble way, let me compensate you as best I can, not only to give you back your self-esteem, but the pleasurable knowledge that as a woman who can inspire passion and adoration, you are surely in the foremost rank."

I heard her sigh and saw her blush more deeply. At last she turned her face tword me, her eyes shimmering with a lovely light through those penitential tears. Her lips trembled as if to speak, and then she glanced down at her slim hand, which was still lying atop my cock, and she gave a little gasp of "Ohhh, how wicked I have suddenly become, and it's all your fault, sir!"

156

I laughed aloud in my joy at seeing her thus happily reconciled to destiny, and I said, "Sweet Marion, give me your lips and let us seal our bargain, our past of peace and companionship henceforth."

She smiled then and nodded, and then my mouth was on hers, gently at first, until I felt the soft, moist petals quiver in acquiescence, and very delicately I advanced the tip of my tongue to hers. She quivered and moaned a little, and her fingers squeezed very slightly my now invigorated cock. Correspondingly, my left hand tightened on the soft thrust of her bubbie, my fingertips brushing the sweet, softly crinkly bud until I felt it turgify. And now my right hand, which had been dallying so gently and lingeringly over first one stockinged thigh and then the other, now boldly marched along the bare olive-sheened skin towards the furry nest between them. With my forefinger, I began to tickle the lips of Marion's soft, moist and quivering cunt.

As she felt that titillation, she groaned a little, and then her arms flung round me and locked me to her as she sank back on the cushions, and the shifting of her beautiful naked body granted me total access to her most secret charms. My forefinger unhesitatingly moved back to find that lodestone of her being, the crux and kernel of all her womanhood. And very gently I began to rub the dainty button of sweet love-flesh, while my tongue foraged more audaciously still inside her nectared mouth.

When at last I released her lips, she was panting and sighing, her thick lashes fluttering wildly, incontrovertable proof that she was withholding nothing from me now and that all hostility and mistrust had vanished. Exhultance filled me, along with eager lust, to know that I had not only de-pedestalled Marion from that lofty and unatainable peak of hatred and contempt to the warm ebullience of communal passion.

"You are not afraid of me any longer, my darling Marion?" I whispered.

She shook her lovely head, closing her eyes and lowering her head demurely.

"Good! Now since I have taken such liberties with your person, it is only fair that you should take equal freedom with mine," I told her. "Explore with that sweet hand and learn the naature of this instrument which rises to your command and droops at your neglect. Constate its powers and its deliverance from ennui and frustrating frigidity. Touch it where and as you will, and learn its portents for that happiness to which nature destined you in giving you so delicious a body—yes, and so sweet and hot and tight a cunt in which to accept my willing weapon!"

She kept her face averted, but nonetheless the lovely brunette began hesitantly and shyly, like a new bride on her eve of wakening, to graze and tickle, to press and squeeze, to explore, to observe the dimensions of my now thoroughly erect phallus.

Her touch was velvety and soft and quivering, perhaps subtly different from Alice's, and so the more enjoyable because of that delicious difference. She was perhaps more inquisitive because, older, she had denied herself so long and been denied in turn, by that wretched Harry to whom I daresay I should be heartily grateful; had he not withered the sprouts of affection in her voluptuous form, I might this afternoon have had no such triumph, a greater one than I had first envisioned when I had first lured her into my Snuggery.

"You must touch my balls too, Marion darling," I instructed her, "for these are the sacks which contain the

158

balm and the balsam of intense pleasure, a panacea to the most reluctant, the driest, the most frigid cunt."

"Is—is that what you call my s-s-spot?" she naively queried, while her cheeks and throat and forehead flamed at her own sweetly scandalous obscenity. I observed the quivering curve of her red, moist lips as she said that naughty, image-provoking word, and my pulses leaped in salacious ecstasy.

"Yes, my dear Marion, that and 'pussy' and 'cunny', too. The more imaginative the lover, the more descriptive his names for that temple of Venus, that grotto of all delight, that haven of exquisite repose and languishing fulfillment," I spoke in a mellow and poetic tone, to bring her still further from that pathway of guilty prurience which one finds in those of little imagination who still believe that the art of fucking should be under a cloud, in the dark and secretive and sinful.

Her fingertips grazed my balls, and they throbbed and ached, telling me that they still contained the wherewithal to offer tribute to my newly acquired mistress. All this while, my finger was touching her clitoris, though I had not been too active, so as not to bring her too quickly to climax. I wished that climax to be shared with me, to seal the bond infrangibly between us. For once thoroughly appeased of all her secret ardors, my beautiful sister-in-law to be would not again hold me in contempt or deem me guilty of insufficient homage to her charms.

But her sweet cunt was moistening, and the love-juices which had been gathering for so long were now readily appearing as Nature graciously showed my beautiful blackhaired *inamorata the* felicitous bounty which comes only with candor and honesty in the way between a man and a maid.

She no longer clutched her thighs so perilously tight, and though her muscles shivered and flexed as I brushed the tender lodestone inside her temple, Marion in no way withheld herself. Once again I kissed her, and this time my tongue was met by her, with a little moaning sigh that welcomed me to take the amorous initiative, knowing it would be met and abetted by my beautiful partner. I left off touching her clitoris to rim the twitching inner lips of her cunt with the tip of my forefinger, and they were swollen and moist with the sweet cream of this prelude to bliss.

"Will you love me now, dear Marion?" I murmured, for now I meant to give her the choice, to let her see she was no longer the slave but freest of lovers, and I waited impatiently to learn whether she had profited by this lesson in the strategy of courtship and of fucking, between prick and cunt, between man and maid.

Oh, how well she had! With a little cry, she flung both her arms around me and dragged me down upon her, my chest mashing down the heaving goblets of her bubbies and her tongue rapiered its way into my own eager mouth. Our tongues thus commenced a friction that was a portent of that greater and more glorious friction soon to be effected between us. I fitted myself to her, and my cockhead rubbed her inner thigh and then prodded at the gates of her domain, imploring entrance. With another little moan of acquiescence, she squirmed a bit, as if to make room for me, and with a shout of joy I felt the tip of my spear probe easily now into her moistened cunt, and as my hands slipped under her bottom to hold her tightly, I felt myself press forward into that gloriously tight channel to the very hilt.

She groaned, her eyes closed, her nostrils flaring wildly, as I slowly drew myself back to the gateway of this paradise of pussy, only to sink back as slowly again till I was buried again to my balls. Her buttocks jerked against my grasp, and their contractions told me there need be no more words between us, only sweet fucking.

Now, withdrawing my right hand, I edged it between us and my forefinger once more sought the button of Marion's clitoris, as I drew back from that charming nook which held my cock so snugly. Indeed, if I was any judge, Marion's cunt was equally as tight as sweet Alice's, which was not surprising since, despite three years of conjugal union to the dolt Harry, she was herself truly a virgin to fucking.

The moment my finger touched her lovebutton again, Marion uttered aloud, "Ohh my Lord! Oh, Jack!" in such a tone of panting rapture and wonderous delight that I shuddered with the afflux of an almost overpowering lust. It was as if she had come upon the gates of paradise itself! Flattening that tumescent nodule with my fingertip, I now thrust myself slowly back down into her depths, and even I was not prepared for the convulsive and frenzied clutching of her arms and of her legs, too—yes, her stockinged thighs and claves coiled over me as might the attacking serpents, pinioning me to her with such ardor that my pulses hammered wildly in sheer erotic joy. My lips met hers, and now our tongues had free coming and going, and I felt her fingernails dig into my tensioned back while under my left palm her naked, velvety bottom weaved and lunged and squirmed uncontrollably.

Back I drew again and again to the brink of her sweet cunt, whilst my forefinger prodded and pushed and flattened her stiffening clitoris. Her moans and sobs and whimpering cries were stifled in my mouth as I drank with savoring relish the onomotopoeia of her mounting rapture.

Now I quickened my gait, and my finger furled and pressed and rolled the stiffening little button; and

Marion could not control her responses as her climax neared. Her legs threshed round me with their feverish lock, her nails gouged my back, her eyes opened and rolled and glazed, while her tongue slashed and stabbed and daggered at me, as she now seemed to thrust up her pelvis to meet my every down-digging plunge. She began to gasp and groan, and her bubbies wildly surged against my dominating chest, flattening their sweet turrets with such a brash exuberance as to belie completely the formidable prudish countenance she had once put on things . . . was it centuries ago?

Then suddenly she twisted her face away, her eyes wild and staring. She arched up her loins just as I thrust to the very hilt, and just as my finger thrust and flattened the love button back into its soft, protective cowl of pink love-flesh, Alice's sister uttered a piercing scream that vibrated in my ears like the heralding of all the angels of heaven: "Ohhh—ahhhhh! Ohhhh, Jack, I am going to die! Oh, Jack, hurry—oh, darling, oh Jack—oh-oh-oh!" And with this she cleaved unto me, our bellies grinding together as I poured forth my last libation of the afternoon and felt it met by the responding torrent of her ecstatic climax-cream.

It was the little death the philosophers write of, and it was renascence for both of us, but most of all for Marion, whose lovely face was contorted in the sweet rictus of passionate fulfillment for what was undoubtedly the first time in all her lovely life.

Chapter *13*

I let her quit me for a much-needed respite in the bidet, while I put back on my silk dressing gown and poured out two glasses of wine, this time without any addition of cantharides to her glass. Seeing me in my dressing gown, she blushed again, and at once put her hand over her mount, murmuring sweetly, "You have the advantage of me again, Jack, so won't you let me put back on my things?"

"Not quite yet, my dear, for your beauty should never be veiled and before you leave, I shall certainly wish to bid you a last tender farewell," I gallantly answered as I handed her her glass. She seated herself on the couch, leaning back, arching out those wonderfully firm bubbies, whose nipples were very definitely darkened and turgified by all the excitement they had met in so short a space of time, concentrtaed into one afternoon and thus acquiring far more experience within that span than she had known throughout her three years of domesticity.

She looked so naughtily wanton in just her stockings that I could not resist rushing over to salute her on the throat and then on each gorgeous bubbie in turn, at which she actually giggled, then blushed divinely. Nonetheless, she crossed her legs one over the other, letting me admire the play of muscles and the firm swelling contours of her uppermost thigh, and then, to distract her from self-consciousness, I remarked, "Did you know that Alice has learned from me how to chastise her maid, Fanny, when the latter is impertinent, as she so often is?"

This struck a responsive cord in Marion's bosom, evidently, for she looked up at me with those dark blue eyes quite wide with surprise, and, shaking her head, replied, "Good heavens, I can hardly believe that, Jack. I have seen Fanny a great deal, as you know, but I never dreamed that my meek little sister could ever dominate her."

"No, because you were such a past mistress at dominating her yourself," I chuckled. She bit her under lip at this and glanced down, and I realized I was on a rather touchy subject, so I hastened on: "But it is quite true, and you have only to ask Alice yourself. Why, she has had Fanny here in the Snuggery, and bound her and tickled her and smacked her—and, I might add, loved her."

"Loved her?" Marion gasped in echo, her eyes wider than ever.

"Why, yes, to be sure. You cannot mean to tell me you have never heard of the art whereby two lovely women can find affection in their own persons?" I chanced.

"No! Assuredly, no. But how can such a thing be?"

Yes, Marion's sexual education had quite evidently been limited, and apparently it was going to fall to me as her initiator to edify her on many subjects. What a pleasant prospect to have before one!

"Yes, it's quite common indeed," I said casually, as I lit a fresh cigar and took a sip of my wine. "There is nothing so strange about it, for it took place thousands of years ago on the Island of Lesbos, when dear Bilitis was the favorite of the priestess Sappho."

"That is all very well," Marion primly remarked, "but it tells me nothing, Jack."

"Is this my former haughty Marion speaking?" I laughed. "Here you are pressing me for the most intimate details and on a still more intimate subject, and only a little while ago you thought me the most contemptible brute and blackguard."

"Oh, please, do forget that, won't you, Jack?" she entreated, and she sent me the most exquisitely appealing glance from those lovely blue eyes.

I could not gainsay her now, after she had proved herself so passionately cooperative on the couch of love, and so I went over and kissed her again on the mouth, and I drew her free hand down toward my dwindled prick as a new test of her compliance. To my delight, she did not withdraw her hand or shrink in the least but instead took hold of my weapon boldly and sweetly stroked the head and 'felt the balls, which had considerably diminished, as one can imagine.

"Well, now," I went on as I seated myself beside her, "the fact simply is, Marion, that girls have as much passion as men, as you yourself have just demonstrated so beautifully—"

At this she drew in her breath sharply, and her blushes deepened. It was delightful to see her like this, almost like a virgin.

"And," I went on as I shifted myself still closer to her, "sometimes some of the bolder and more ardent females even try to duplicate nature by artificial means to make up for the absence of that which you are so delightfully touching now."

At this she drew her hand away from my cock, but I seized her wrist and drew it back to my cock, for I was beginning to appreciate her caresses. I did not think myself capable of still another spend, for I thought I had given her all my essence, but if we went on this way I could well chance the strenuous taxation on my vigor by assaying further amorous passages with this delectable young woman.

"Whatever do you mean, you wicked man?" she said with another slurred little giggle. "I knew it was a dreadful mistake as soon as I walked into your apartment, and now I am more convinced of it than ever."

"But not nearly so unhappy about it as when you first did, eh?" I whispered, and she blushed and nodded. "Well then," I said as I finished my wine and set the glass down, "it is really quite elementary. And there are numerous ways in which women can make love together, just as there are between ourselves. For example, one may lie upon the other and with their arms about them, each will kiss and rub back and forth to create the most diverting friction and passionate glow imaginable in their sweet cunts."

"Ohh my!" Marion gasped at this illuminating edification, and I saw the rosy hue of her cheeks grow even more fiery as she averted her face from me.

"And then, they may wish to use their mouths and tongues, as I did with you when you were standing there, so pretty, with arms held high above your head and legs spread apart so you could not resist my blandishments," I continued.

"Oh dear! If you ever dare breath a word to Alice, I—I don't know what I'll do!" she tremulously confessed. I held her hand tightly now against my cock, and I leaned over to kiss her sweet rosy mouth.

"The time will come," I murmured, "when you will tell her everything yourself, and for pleasure, mark my words, Marion."

"Oh, I should never dare! What would Alice think of me, after I have treated her so severely?" she breathed.

"As I was going to say," I resumed my didactic lecture, "they may emulate my example with you by placing themselves in reverse over each other, and while one kisses and tongues the soft cunt of the other, the latter in turn requites her in kind. And then again, there are those who are passive by nature, and wish to have love made to them but wish someone else to take the initiative. So as you were lying on the couch a little while ago, the other girl will simply kneel between her thighs and kiss and lick and suck her there."

"Do you mean, Jack, that Alice and Fanny do those things together?" She stared directly at me, and her eyes were huge as saucers.

"I rather think they do, but again, as I told you, you can learn all this from Alice simply by consulting with her," I said slyly.

"Jack! Now you are being too bold! If I were to do such a thing, do you not think Alice would at once guess what had happened between us today?"

"I rather think she would, for your sister is almost as alert and vivacious of mind as yourself, Marion," I praised her. "That is why you must deliberate as to the wisdom of taking the bull by the horns and telling her yourself, in a manner which will turn it to your own best advantage."

"But to get back to Fanny and Alice," Marion pursued, for evidently this was piquing her quite a good deal, "you know, I have a maid also who is in my opinion certainly more impertinent than Fanny on many occasions, and I have been beside myself to know what tack to take with her to teach her more deference and humility."

"I will make the same offer to you that I made to Alice before you," I chuckled. "Bring her here and enlist my aid, and between the two of us, we will teach this saucy baggage her place, my dear."

"Good heavens, I couldn't do that! But still—"

"But still?" I questioned as I kissed her left nipple, taking it between my lips and flicking it with the tip of my tongue till she moaned with pleasure.

"Now, you're not—not to do that anymore, because I am all quieted down now and you mustn't drive me giddy again so soon," my sweet brunette *inamorata* chided. But from a delicious glint in her eyes and the sudden erratic heaving of her gorgeous bubbies, I could see I had not at all displeased her by my attentions.

"You are begging the question again, you impertinent minx, and you know what that will cost your bottom if you persist in it," I teased her.

"Oh, that was so humiliating I don't dare think of it. Please, don't let's speak of it," Marion stammered, blushing. "But you were saying about Kay—that is my maid's name—that you and I could together make her toe the mark. Why, do you know what she did yesterday afternoon?"

"I haven't the slightest notion, Marion dear."

"Well, I wanted her to run an errand for me, you see," Marion earnestly began, "and the saucy vixen had the temerity to tell me that she was already occupied with laying out my clothes for dinner last night and she certainly would not have time for such a commission."

"And you didn't even box her ears for her?"

"Heavens, no, she is as tall as I am and quiet determined in her ways."

"And so am I, unless you have by chance forgotten it," I said with a mocking little smile, at which she colored and lowered her eyes. "Decidedly this Kay needs a good birching or bottomsmacking to teach her manners to her mistress. And as your new protector, Marion, I herewith engage myself to that task. You will enjoy assisting me, I am certain."

"You mean, you would tie her up as you tied me, and then—"

168

"And then disrobe her? I would indeed, with your permission, to be sure."

"Oh, Jack! It would be delightful. And she does have it coming, the impertinent hussy!"

"How old is this paragon of virtue of yours?"

"Twenty-three, and she leads the poor hostlers and clerks a merry chase, from all she tells me. Why, do you know, she boasts openly of flirting, and then when these unhappy men make overtures to her, scoring them off, and she boasts of it to me."

"She is what the French call a *demi-vierge,* a half-virgin, who enjoys using her powers of allure to agonize and frustrate her victims. Decidedly, she is in need of a good lesson, Marion."

"Then, Jack, I will bring her to you tomorrow afternoon. Oh dear, what time is it? I must go, really I must, dear Jack.

She tried to rise from the couch, but my hands were cupping her bubbies and it was no easy task. My lips once more met hers, and now I felt my cock throb and stiffen in a last farewell manifestation of its hunger for Marion's sweet, hot, encompassing flesh. I kissed her on the mouth and let my tongue roam at will, and she answered as avidly as I. My hands slipped down from her breasts to caress the insides of her olive-sheened upper thighs, and soon I had my forefinger on the twitching lips of her cunt again and was delving to find the clitoris.

Marion's breath came quickly now, erratically, and she moaned and tried to clench her thighs together. But my finger had taken its inroads and it was already far too late for her to make such a defensive manoeuver. Squirming on that lovely bottom of hers, leaning back, her eyes closed, she moaned as my finger plied her love-button with the most insidious touchings and caresses.

"And one thing more, Marion," I remarked as I ended

a long, passionate kiss which left her quivering in my arms, "once you have helped me strip and smack this naughty maid of yours, you can, if you wish, reconcile yourself with her in the manner I have just described, and she will be your sweet prisoner of love."

"Oh dear Heavens! What you say is so outlandish and naughty that I ought to be terribly vexed with you," she panted, but again the flash in her dark blue eyes would have me believe that she did not find my words so terrible after all.

At last I allowed the beautiful naked brunette to rise from the couch to dress again, to dress and to be free of me. I watched her, for to see a female restore her clothes to order over her naked beauty has always been for me one of the choicest regalia of this life.

"My blouse and my bodice and the front of my dress will hardly hold together after your outrageous treatment," she chided me, with a hasty glance in my direction.

"I will lend you a cape to put over you to hide the disarray, and I shall keep my word as to replacing that pretty frock. My sister-in-law to be must surely accept a present of friendship which it will be my pleasure to offer you. You will go to the Sandys Salon on Fleet Street and have them send the bill to me for anything you wish."

"Oh, how nice you are now, and how I had misjudged you, Jack!" she cried ecstatically as she clung her arms around my neck and hugged me. My right hand continued to forage in the sweet region of her cunt, while my left hand at the back of her neck forced her panting, most, warmly red mouth against my lips.

At last I escorted her to the door of my apartment, and it was a far different Marion that I led there than I had let enter. Now she was an arch-conspiratress who was destined to bring into my life new pleasures and delights, and who would not now stand in the way of my happiness with Alice.

Chapter *14*

Unhappily, the next day a messenger came round with a note from Marion saying that she regretted not being able to keep our tentative assignation, but my heart bounded with joy when I read the postscript which she had added:

"I think if all goes well you may expect a visit from me tomorrow afternoon, and I shall take my maid shopping with me."

History was about to repeat itself! How well I remembered the exquisite way in which my beloved Alice had taken to the bait of demonstrating that she, too, could couple sweet sadism to love's alluring ways and brought vivacious Fanny to my Snuggery. In so doing, naturally, as you, my patient readers, no doubt remember, she had offered me an additional *inamorata* for my private harem, the incomparable Fanny. Not only that, this introduction had resulted in a sweet *rapport* between Fanny and her young mistress, so I may be said to have diversely contributed to the happiness of others than myself, and thus could not be charged with the epithet of selfish, unprincipled rogue and bachelor *roue*.

Via the same messenger, whom I tipped handsomely, I sent back an answering note that I should be quite at Marion's disposal the following afternoon, and I bade the energetic young man who had conveyed this message to execute a further commission for me by pausing on his way back to Marion at a florist's and there purchasing a dozen dark red roses with which my card was to be enclosed.

I dined at Simpson's that evening to replenish my vigor, which I foresaw I should sorely need when not only Marion herself but the intrepid Kay, whom I had not once met, should visit my Snuggery. In my dreams that night, as you may well expect, were full of the most titillating and lascivious scenes and images as my fertile dalliance and voluptuous chastisements which I proposed to inflict not only upon Kay but opon her mistress as well.

All my preparations were made and the apartment was in excellent order. I lunched early, ordering a glass of wine to drink a solitary toast to the oncoming pleasures, and then I waited with impatience. The doorbell rang at two o'clock.

I was immaculately dressed, as I had been when I received Marion, and when I opened the door, my eyes widened with admiration. Standing just behind Marion, who wore an entrancingly attractive blue frock and a dainty matching bonnet, was a young woman as tall, perhaps more svelte, with a profusion of coppery-red curls and the most impertinently sulky face one can imagine. With dainty snub nose, insolent and very ripe mouth, high-set cheekbones and a complexion of pale ivory flecked by tiny rosy dots, the genuine and ardent complexion of a true redhead. Her eyes were gray-green and very closely set together, while her lashes were extremely long and thick and her eyebrows full and eloquent. I looked forward to testing whether her mercurial nature and secret amorous proclivities were in keeping with her spirited and sensually enticing countenance.

"Well, a pleasant afternoon to you, Jack," Marion

174

blithely greeted me. "I was out shopping and found myself nearby, so I asked our driver to let us off here, so that I can thank you for those beautiful flowers. How thoughtful you were, Jack."

"It was my pleasure," I bowed low, "and it was only a humble tribute to your beauty and warmth."

I saw the redhaired maid prick up her ears at this, and she shot me a covert glance full of mischief and malice. *Aha,* I thought to myself, *I know the cut of your jib well enough already, my fine wench!* Yes, this Kay was the sort who would spy on her mistress to gain a hold over her, and I knew she was specualting on what might have passed between us for me to have addressed Marion in so warm a manner and for Marion to reply to me in kind. Well, I should soon disabuse her of this unjustified status-seeking, I told myself, as I invited Marion to enter my domain.

I asked her if she would not take a cup of tea with me and Marion gratefully acquiesced, graciously inviting Kay to share with us, but the pert wench tossed her head and tartly replied, "No thank you, ma'am. I'll wait till high tea, if you don't mind."

Marion's eyes met mine and I saw a sort of facial expression on her charming features which told me this was quite typical of the maid. Ah, the wench was overdue for chastisement, months ago.

"As you like," I said airily, "but at least, since I am a mere man, you may be gracious, Kay, to help me prepare the tea exactly the way your mistress wishes it."

She came forward with a sort of sulky resignation, and I watched her handle my tea things with summary dispatch. I said nothing, but I glanced again at Marion, who smiled and nodded. Yes, I had her approbation in my proposed scheme of thing, and judging from tne grimace of annoyance she made when Kay placed her

175

cup before her with an annoying clatter of the saucer, I was sure she would give me not only moral support but also physical assistance when it came to the disciplinary measures I meant to take with this coppery-haired young vixen.

I recalled only too well how Alice and I had conspired to bring Fanny along that memorable afternoon, how the two of us had administered a voluptuous chastisement to the darkharied maid, who is now as thoroughly impassioned as my beloved sweetheart. But Fanny at least had had a redeeming demureness and sweet humility, even with all her persiflage, whereas my impression of redhaired Kay was that she was spoiling for the rod in pickle, to turn a phrase. I did not know how long Marion had had her in service, but it was evident at once that she lacked the proper breeding for being a discreet *confidante* between a man and a maid of higher social plateau than her own. So I resolved that while providing Marion with her debut as a loving flagellant, I should requite on my own account this saucy baggage's brash manner, not only toward her mistress during the episode of tea, but also toward myself. I saw that Marion was somewhat ill at ease, obbiously not knowing how to proceed in making this debut which would once and for all proclaim her superiority and dominance over her redhaired vixen of a maid, so I deemed it meet to commence the proceedings.

"There is something I should like you to examine, Marion," I soberly remarked, "because I, being a bachelor, cannot be expected to know much about decor, and I have probably committed several errors in taste and judgment."

"I should be happy to give what little advice I can, Jack," Marion flushed as she replied in a low voice, "but you must realize that since Harry and I have been separated, I have had little occasion to think of such relatively inconsequential matters as furnishing and decorating."

"Surely you are not a recluse yet, my dear," I jokingly replied with twinkling eyes, "for you are far too young and lovely to sequestrate yourself in a mausoleum and hide your charms from an appreciative society."

I saw Kay give her mistress an almost sneering look at this, and I could scarecely contain myself with glee because it was obvious at once that this impertinent creature dared censure her betters. I blandly urged Marion, therefore, to come with me into what I termed my "photographic salon" so that I might have her valuable opinion. She did so, and, glancing back over her shoulder, casually added, "come along, Kay, please."

"If you don't mind, ma'am, I'll stay here. I'm sure you'd just as soon prefer that anyhow," was the bold jade's pert answer. Marion's face flamed, because the maid's quip was an arrow shot far too close for comfort, and she looked at me helplessly, hoping I could right the situation.

I eyed Kay with a crushing glance and thereupon remarked, "Do you know, Marion, I wonder how long you have had this sharp-tongued young woman in your service, for it she were in my employ, she would receive a week's notice for such an insolent answer."

"But I'm not, sir, and I'll thank you not to address your remarks to me," was Kay's insolent retort, as with flashing eyes and scornful features she pulled herself up. Decidedly she was playing right into my hands, which fairly itched to deal her out the sort of chastisement her audacity fully merited.

"Now this is quite enough, Kay," Marion said sharply, and she was not playing a part now. "I wish you to accompany me, and you will do so. Do you understand?"

"Very well, if you put it that way, ma'am," Kay drawled with as condescending an air as she could muster.

And so the time had come, and I forced myself to keep my features grave and controlled so that our intended victim could not have the faintest inkling what awaited her inside that door which led to my "photographic salon!"

Once inside, I slipped back to turn the spring lock which was so well concealed that a stranger to the Snuggery could never locate it in a time of aggravated haste, and then casually I led the way.

"Do you not think, Marion," I sententiously demanded, "that it is much too dark and gloomy in here?"

"But for the development work you must do, Jack, I should say it is quite in keeping. But do, pray, tell me what are all those curious pillars and the rings fixed to them?" Marion innocently asked.

"Why, I should say they were there to guarantee the docility and obedience of insolent baggages," I blandly countered, as I turned to look at Kay. "And if you like, I should be happy to demonstrate to you just how effective they can be."

I had, as I passed by the panel on the wall, slyly touched the button which lowered the rope-pulleys, those same aids which had enabled me to subjugate delicious Alice, so they were now at easy reach when the moment came to entrap the redhaired minx who had incited both of us to irritation with her.

"Are you speaking to me, sir?" Kay indignantly exclaimed, drawing herself up again and tightening her lips with evident displeasure.

"I was indeed addressing you, Kay," I rejoined, "and since your mistress does not have the spunk or perhaps

178

the hardness of heart necessary to correct your intolerable behavior, I shall take it upon myself to do so."

With this, striding towards her and taikng her entirely by surprise, for her mouth gaped and her eyes went very wide indeed, I seized her by a wrist and dragging it up to the nearest pulley, in a trice had fastened her securely, while I called to Marion to emulate me on the other side.

"What are you doing—how dare you treat me like this, and you, too, ma'am—oh, you'll both be sorry for this, you mark my words!" Kay stormed as she tugged at her bound wrists and kicked out at us both. She did indeed succeed in barking Marion's shin, rather lightly but enough to make my beautiful brunette sister-in-law to be absolutely furious with her. I was really grateful to the baggage for having thus forced her mistress's hand, for now there was no doubt whatsoever that Marion would heartily abet me in my imminent plans for the thorough chastisement of this wretchedly impertinent and forward young vixen.

Going to the wall, I touched a button to elevate Kay's arms overhead, till she was forced to stand on tiptoe, the while she shrieked her angry denunciations of us both. I took no heed of these at all, needless to say, but warily approaching her on her right, squatted down behind her and in a trice bound her slender ankle with a silken rope and made it fast to the pillar. Marion, with quick native wit, followed my example with almost as much dexterity as if she had done this sort of thing all her life.

Thus in a few moments we had the raging, redhaired baggage secured, ready for disrobing and the subsequent punishment which would follow.

"Now then, Marion," I said calmly, as we both stood back to observe the furious, writhing captive, "do you not agree that this minx deserves a sound birching?"

Indeed she does!" Marion retorted with a sparkling

glint in her eyes which boded no good for her maid. "You don't know how I've wanted to take her down a peg or two, Jack. She's been in my service eighteen months now, and I am certain the way she's flouted me had not a little to do with dear Harry's becoming vexed with me and—"

"That's a lie!" Kay cried out hoarsely, beside herself with fury as she tugged uselessly at her bound wrists tied high above her head. "Anyone with half an eye could see from the start that you couldn't keep that nice husband of yours, so you just wanted to take it out on me. I could tell you, how extravagant you were and—"

"That's quite enough, Kay," I broke in sternly. "You are only aggravating your already considerable case against your mistress. I am no judge of what happened between the two of you outside of my abode, but this I can tell you: the way you have acted toward us both this afternoon is itself enough to condemn you to rebuke many times over."

"And what, sir, do you intend to do, sir?" Kay sneered. "When you let me go—as you're going to have to, you know—I shall go to a constable and have you taken in charge for this outrageous insult."

"Well, then, Marion, since you seem determined to charge us rather more seriously than we have already acted, do you not suppose we may as well merit the charge?" I turned to the beautiful brunette beside me.

Marion's eyes shone, and she murmured, "Oh yes, Jack, I'm dying to see her come down off her high horse and start realizing her place!"

"Then why don't you undress her and get her ready for the birch!" I asked, loudly enough to be heard by our proposed victim. Kay could not believe her ears.

"What? What did you just say? Birch me? You wouldn't, you wouldn't dare! Oh, I should like to see you try, I should! You'd dearly regret it if you lay a finger on me, I can tell you that!"

"It will not be a finger, but a good swishy birch, Kay, administered judiciously and soundly across your naked posterior," was my cold answer.

"Oh, let me do it, Jack," Marion gasped, her bosom rising and falling with excitement.

"She is your maid, after all, so it is only just that you should deliver her up to punishment," I gallantly rejoined.

"At last!" Marion exclaimed, as she approached the horrified redhead, who until this very moment could not believe the testimony of her ears and eyes.

"No—I forbid you to—you shan't—sir, are you going to let her undress me in your presence? This is indecent, outrageous, vile!"

"Not one twentieth part so vile as your sly insinuations about your mistress and her husband," was my cold answer, "and if your modesty should be offended, you have only yourself to blame for it. Meanwhile, I shall go fetch the birch."

I had cut two fresh birch rods that morning, one thin, long and very flexible, the other somewhat bulkier, binding them with a cloth strip to serve as handle and arranging them most expertly for the proper castigation of a female bottom. To be sure, the choice would be decided by the victim's proportions, so one may judge with what impatience I awaited Marion's preparations.

Marion lost no time. First unbuttoning the straps of Kay's plain muslin dress, she dragged the garment down to the girl's waist. Then she unbuttoned Kay's undervest, leaving the redhead in only her chemise, which covered bosom and loins. This was not done, however, without frenzied threatening, shrieking and struggling, as Kay, absolutely frantic at the shameful thought of being undressed before a man, flung herself this way and that against her bonds.

"You will not be able to get her frock off without releasing her feet, Marion," I suggested, "and I daresay you do not wish to do that since she is the mulish sort who will kick. Here, take this pair of scissors and cut it off her."

"Oh, you miserable scoundrel, to do such a thing to a helpless girl," Kay cried hysterically as she tried to lunge backwards as she saw Marion approach, scissors in hand. "Help me, for the Lord's sake! Sir, sir, how can you stand there and let this happen to a defenseless girl, a decent girl who's never done any harm to anyone in all her life?"

"I would not be surprised if you had quite a bit to do with harming Marion's marriage," I sternly replied, "but your mistress has asked for my aid and I am here to give it. You will have to appeal to her, I am afraid."

By now Marion had cut the frock off and dragged it away, and now the undervest had been removed and Kay stood there in only her batiste chemise, her gray cotton stockings and plain black shoes. But that *deshabille* was already breathtaking enough to set my cock to aching and stirring in its dormant hiding place.

She was magnificently svelte, and in some ways even more sinuous and supple than her mistress. Demurely cut as the chemise was it did not in the least dissemble the splendid promonitories of her bosom, high-perched globes shaped somewhat like ripe pears, set widely apart and hrusting their voluptuously developed buds vigorously against the stuff of her chemise. From her slim waist there flared a pair of delectably sleek, agile hips, and her buttocks were broad ovals with a gradually widening furrow between them. Her thighs were delightfully long and almost boyishly slender.

"Oh, ma'am, no—for God's sake, not in front of him! Have mercy on me!" Kay exclaimed, as she lunged back and tried to escape her mistress's reach. But I stood there with hands clasped behind my back enjoying the spectacle of this embattled vixen at bay and the still more exquisite scene of the once arrogant Marion's playing the role of executioner. The buttons fell one by one to Marion's nimble fingers, and now she moved to Kay's other side, ignoring the girl's sobbing pleas as she undid those as well. The chemise suddenly descended, falling to Kay's hips, exposing those beautiful bubbies in all their glory.

"Ohhh! Oh my God, oh my God, cover me up, ma'am, I beg of you, not in front of him—don't let him see me n-naked!" and already the anger in her voice had given way to real shame and terror, the two most voluptuously rousing emotions a man can discern in a proposed female captive.

Those bubbies were wonderfully firm and uptilting, with narrow, dark coral aureolae, and extremely well-developed nipples. Her navel, also, was a jewel in the flesh, very dainty, deep and very narrow, and in the frenzied play of her muscles as she threw herself this way and that against her bonds, it seemed to wink at me as if inviting me to pay its owner ardent tribute—which I surely meant to do.

The chemise would go no lower, owing to the straddle of her legs. Marion seized at the folds of the garments and tugged at them, ignoring Kay's piteous pleas for mercy, but found the progress impeded. Again to my delight, without being told, she resorted to the scissors and then I uttered a gasp of unconcealed admiration as the garment fell to the floor and Kay stood exposed, naked except for the stockings, before us both.

The silky thatch at the juncture of her thighs was ex-

183

tremely thick and of a darker, more auburn shade than the hair of her lovely arrogant head. She was, to be truthful, even more thickly furred than her mistress, whose public foliage I have already intimately described.

Discovering herself so shamelessly unveiled, Kay closed her eyes, turned her face to one side, and desperately tugged at her bound wrists, shrieking wordless plaints and madly trying to clench her thighs, so the muscles stood out under the satiny pale, milky skin of her thighs.

I now went to the closet and brought back both birch rods, one in each hand—the bulkier in my left. My preference was for the lighter one, for though Kay's bottom was spacious, it had that compact, sinuous quality to it that fairly cried out for a thinner, swishier rod.

My own, rod, as you may well guess by this time, was violently turgid, but I made no effort to conceal my protuberance from Kay's dilated, horrified eyes. I turned to Marion now, handing her the birch in my right hand and remarking, "I believe you will find this birch ideally suited to her insolent posterior."

"Oh, it looks as if it will really sting her properly, Jack," Marion exalted, as she took it in her right hand, brandishing it about with many a vicious swish in the air, under the eyes of the now thoroughly frightened maid.

"You surely aren't going to hit me with that dreadful thing! Oh, sir, please don't let her beat me—she's got such a terrible temper, you've no idea. She'll cut me to ribbons, I know she will."

"And so you richly deserve, you sharp-tongued, maliciously gossiping baggage," I irritatedly retorted. "I will not lift a finger to help you." (Nor, dear reader, would I, but I was already lifting my prick in tribute to this redhaired hussy about to pass under the birch for the first time.)

Taking her place behind Kay, Marion called out to me, "How many do you think I should give her, Jack?"

"Why, as to that, dear, let your conscience be your guide," I laughingly retorted. "But mind you, lay them on slowly so she will have ample time to feel the effects of each good stroke. You will also find the lower part of her bottom is much more sensitive to a birch like that, which cuts and stings and draws, than the upper region. Also, listen carefully to her assuredly vivid descriptions of what she is undergoing, which will give you a much-needed clue as to what quota you may set for this her first flogging."

"Oh, you heartless, you dreadful man, to stand by and le me so brutally treated. No, no—oh, for God's sake, sir, have pity!"

"I have already told you I am *hors de concours*," I taunted her. "This dispute is between your mistress and yourself, so address your supplications and your jeremiads to her entirely."

"Now then, Miss," Marion addressed her as she laid the swishy rod full across the fleshiest curves of her maid's clenching and trembling naked bottomcheeks, "I am going to teach you manners, I am, and you are not going to get off very lightly. Kick me in the shins, would you? Tell me that my husband sought your advice about me, would you? You shall repent your insolence, my girl, to the very fullest."

With this, after patting Kay's naked bottom a few times, she drew back her right arm and made the birch sing out a doleful *huissshhhish* in the air as the half-dozen freshly cut birch switches swept magistrally across both huddling cheeks of Kay's milky, rosy-flecked bottom.

With a piercing cry of pain, Kay lunged forward and offered the furry gate of her cunt to my blazing eyes. It was all I could do to keep from reaching out and squeezing those heaving bubbies of hers, or caressing her naked belly, or inserting a finger under all those shaggy, dark-red curls to find the delicious inlet to her female secrets.

A second cut now fell, and Kay shrieked aloud, glancing back as she lunged forward, the pulleys creaking under the strain.

"Hold off a bit now, Marion," I advised. "You're going about it much too quickly. Besides, we should put the mirror in front of Kay so she will be prepared for the next cut."

In a few moments I had the huge mirror standing in front of the naked redhead, just as I had done with Marion so recently. The distracted, frantic, naked sufferer perceived herself in the mirror and stared, observing the thickly ringletted fleece between her straddled thighs, and with a gasp of shame, tried with all her powers to clench her thighs and hide that enticing nook from my view.

I now went behind the redhead to observe Marion's handiwork. The very first two cuts of that slim, whippy rod had left angry, bright pink streaks across both Kay's quivering, clenching buttocks; and the vivid, lascivious sight of these stigmata on that wonderfully milky-pale skin of hers was absolutely devastating to my carnal instincts. Her back was deeply hollowed and her shoulders slim and graceful, while the suppleness of her limbs and muscles thoroughly entranced me. If Marion had not been present, I fear I should have deferred Kay's birching for a most gratifying interlude which had as its aim the determination of her virginity, of which state I had, needless to say, no present knowledge.

"Excellent, my dear," I approved, "but take care not to

hurry the cuts and to keep this naughty minx waiting in suspense for each. The proper effect of a good birching is to augment from moment to moment the burning sting of the cut just inflicted, so that the naughty culprit will feel even more apprehensive over the one to follow. And remember my injunction that the underpart of her big bottom is likely to be far more sensitive than the upper region."

"Oh, you hateful, shameless ruffian," Kay tearfully sobbed, as she turned her head back over shoulder to regard me, "you go beyond propriety and decency in this! Oh, I will make you pay for the outrage to my person and to my modesty—I will—Owwww!"

In the midst of her tirade, I had made a gesture to Marion, who had promptly regaled the redhaired baggage with a brisk slash just over the base of both flinching nether globes. Taken by surprise, Kay lunged forward with a wild cry of pain, and the play of her muscles and the jerking of her thighs, together with the contractions of her buttocks, blended together into the most sensual choreography in all the world.

"Now that was excellently done, Marion. And she has just demonstrated the truth of what I advised. Concentrate on the lower curves of that impertinent posterior, and you will be amazed in the transformation in this unruly creature!" I remarked.

I could tell that Marion was entering into the spirit of the game, and with bosom heaving and eyes sparkling, she planted herself like a veteran flagellatress, turned somewhat sideways and at Kay's left, whilst she now patted her maid's shrinking, naked seat with the swishy, long, supple rod as if to intimate where the next stroke would be applied. Kay caught her breath and groaned, steeling herself, whereupon Marion drew back

187

her arm and lunged it forward with full strength. The twigs whisked around to the right, towards the victim's groin, and Kay again shouted in anguish under that slashing cut. Her skin was quite well marked by now, and it was most sensitive and delicate, I saw.

"Oh, how delicious this is—to be able to punish her as she deserves, the spiteful jade," Marion murmured to me as she sent me a humid look of happy gratitude. Then, glancing down at my person, she blushingly whispered, "And you, sir, have a rod in store for my maid, I see, instead of for me!"

What boundless delight these words inspired in me, dear reader, you may well imagine! I could not have dreamed of so perfect a conversion as I had made in this so-apt pupil in fucking and flogging, for look you, she had, in one bound and in that single phrase, told me she would permit me to enjoy the charms of her maid as well as herself.

"But you will always have first preference," I murmured back ingratiatingly.

With a soft laugh, Marion swept another whistling cut, this time across the tops of Kay's straddled thighs, the switches licking greedily at the pale, soft skin just above the founcy, white satin-elastic rosette garters which held her stockings in place on her long, lovely legs.

"Aiii! Oh, for God's sake, will you stop now?" Kay cried in a strident voice. "It is brutal, it is cowardly, to beat a helpless, decent girl like this and to have a man stand by and gloat over her shameful nakedness."

"You should have thought of that before you gave yourself such airs my girl," Marion sanctimoniously responded, and inflicted yet another whistling cut of the flexible rod, this time biting home across the upper summits of Kay's shuddering, naked bottomcheeks and

188

drawing a hoarse, sobbing cry of "Oh, for God's sake, have mercy. You're cutting me to pieces. Stop, I pray you, stop!"

Chapter 15

Marion paused now, exhilirated by this fascinating new sport, finding it no doubt a joyous change to wield the rod instead of herself being the wielder's victim. Then, stepping back a pace or two to give herself more room, she swept the birch from right to left, and holding it at about the level of her own hip, swished it venomously across the tops of Kay's naked behind. Again the tethered captive lunged forward, her thighs shuddering and trying to clench, and her cry was piercing in its intensity:

"Eeeeooowwwwll For Lord's sake, sir, make her stop now, that's quite enough nowl Oh dear, I know I'm bleedingl"

"You are prone to exaggeration as well as to insolence, my girl," I mockingly observed, "for the skin is nowhere broken and, judging by your mistress's surprising skill on her very first essay, I should judge that your naughty backside can stand a good many more such vigorous cuts before there is the slightest tear in yoir impudent skin. You are, I believe, so calloused morally and temperamentally as to have the same imperviousness to pain as you do the infiltration of humility and proper manners in a domestic!"

Marion huskily laughed with delight at this sarcastic little speech, and as I finished it, she loosed yet another stroke of the birch full over the ripest curves of her maid's squirming and writhing bottomcheeks, eliciting another piteous wail and a frantic lunging from side to side, till the rope-pulleys creaked in protest.

"Perhaps," Marion declared, "this will help teach you not to go about carrying tales of my private affairs, my girl!"

And with this, she administered still another whisking slash of the birch just where the base of Kay's voluptuous naked behind merged into the ripe, jouncy contours of the summits.

"Aiiii! Ohh Lord, oh dear, oh sir, sir, for God's sake get her to stop before she kills me, I can't endure such torture, truly I can't!" And again Kay turned her tearstained face back over her shoulder as she sought a reprieve from me for this exemplary chastisement.

"Will you stop that caterwauling, my girl, before I really give you something to squeal about?" Marion angrily demanded, "I have hardly begun to chastise you as you deserve, you spiteful, talebearing baggage!"

"Oh dear heaven, did you hear that, sir? She won't be content until she has killed me. Oh, do make her stop, I implore you!" Kay sobbingly pleaded, her eyes very big and blurred with tears, as once again she turned her head to appeal to me for mercy.

"I will say only that when next you bare your tail, you had best not antagonize your mistress as you have so injudiciously done already," I could not resist from punning. Then, to Marion, I urged, "But pray continue, my dear sister-in-law to be, for I begin to perceive you are making some headway at last, for she is beginning to feel the cuts."

"I would say it was more a case of 'tailway'," to my great delight Marion showed herself to be as deft a punster, thereby indicating her evident relish for this exquisite little game, as again she patted her maid's naked, well-streaked posterior with the swishiest rod.

"Oh, how can you be so wickedly inhuman and merciless, sir, to let a poor, helpless girl suffer like this?" Kay sobbingly asked, and her body lunged forward again, bending like a bow, to escape the dire inclinations of the rod. "I only wish it was she who was getting this instead of me, for she'd be begging off from the very first cut and —aaarrrhhhh! Ohh, mercy, mercy, you're tearing me to shreds. Oh, do have mercy and stop now, for Lord's sake!"

Her sobbing declaration was suddenly cut off as Marion slashed the birch with a quick and brisk maneuver which licked round Kay's satiny right hip and on towards the most intimate part of all her body.

"I should not deafen other people with such braying sounds," Marion sarcastically retorted, and, growing more vehement by the moment as she found sensual excitement in her sport, administered a backhanded cut of the rod from left to right which sent the twigs whistling over the top of Kay's left hip whilst the solid portion of the switches made stinging impact against the top of the minx's left buttock and leaped across to visit the other cheek with an equally ardent salutation.

"Owww! Oh dear, oh, I shall faint, I am beside myself with pain. Oh, sir, what must I do to have you beg me off? Oh dear lord, such torture for a poor, helpless girl. It is unjust and cruel indeed," Kay lamented. Her head lifted and then bowed, she dragged on her wrist-ropes incessantly, and her now vividly striped naked backside jerked and weaved and twisted and squirmed, presenting my enchanted eyes with a most voluptuous vision in the famous and infallibly prick-hardening "dance of the rod."

"Are you ready to apologize for all your nastiness, my

192

girl?" her mistress queried. To hasten Kay's reply, she vengefully cut away at the base of her naked bottom with a whistling, swishing stroke.

"Eeeowwwl! Oh, yes! Oh, please, ma'am, do have mercy. I'm sorry if I angered you, truly I am. Oh, won't you stop now before you kill me?"

"And do you promise never, never again to make such a show of insolence and overbearing impudence when you accompany me to Mr. Jack's apartment or anywhere else I choose to go?" Marion persisted, and this query too she punctuated with a slash of the rod that fairly danced off Kay's bare, jouncy bottom, this in diagonal fashion to bridge the quaking, flinching nether hemispheres and to leave a bright, angry weal on the fine, creamy skin already so piteously marred by stripes and darkening little splotches where the harsher knots at certain sections of the withes had made pitiless impact with that fair flesh.

"Ahhhrrrr! Oh, truly I will, truly I'll know my place, I swear it, ma'am, only do stop, I can't bear any more—oh, I can't, I can't! Oh, Mr. Jack, do make her stop now—I'll be good—I won't give offense ever again, you may be sure of it, sir!"

"I rather think she has had her due from you, my dear Marion," I now interceded, "and besides, my dear, you are out of breath and very flushed. Do you sit down in that convenient chair and rest yourself a bit."

Marion handed me the rod with a long, panting sigh of pleasure, and judging from the humid glow in her dark blue eyes and the quivering of her moist red lips, as well as the heaving of her superb bosom, she had quite enjoyed herself as a practitioner of the rod.

"Are you going to let her down now, Jack dear?" she asked as she seated herself in the chair which had been pulled up to the right of the tethered maid, enabling her to view both back and front of the captive.

"Why, not yet at all," was my answer, "for although you have settled your score with this saucy baggage, I still have one of my own to settle with her."

With this, I moved around to face the aghast redhead who, seeing the dreadful instrument of her suffering gripped firmly in my right hand, let out a pitiful wail of: "Oh my Lord, surely not more whipping? Oh, sir, I apologize to you, truly I do—oh, do forgive me now and spare me. I am at the end of my endurance!"

"Not at all, my girl," was my sardonic retort, "for I do not propose to birch your insolent backside. The rest of you, however, is quite untouched and will provide ample terrain for our little reckoning."

At this, I extended the rod and patted her across the tops of her naked thighs, very near that dark-red thatched mound which was the temple of her young womanhood.

Kay stared down at the rod with a horrified incredulity and then, with a mad lunge backwards, threw back her head and shrieked, "Oh heavens—oh, surely you won't whip me there? Oh, sir, be merciful now, I beg you humbly for forgiveness!"

"I shall accept your supplication only after you have had your chastisement, as that will guarantee that you will keep your promise of better conduct in the future," was my answer.

Drawing back my arm, I lightly made the flexible rod dart across those shaking, distended, creamy upper columns of Kay's delicious thighs and was rewarded by her frenzied twisting and lunging and her harassed scream of "Eeeowwww! Oh, it is dreadful there—oh, please it hurts me worse, sir, far worse—oh, Mr. Jack, do be kind and pardon me any more—I can't stand it, sir."

"But you will just have to stand it till I am satisfied," I gloated, as again I laid the rod just above the tops of her stockings and watched her squirm and shrink, her eyes huge with anguish, drowned with tears which began to rivulet down her cheeks.

"I think before I proceed further," I remarked, "I shall have your stockings down, as they furnish rather too much protection for the whipping of your thighs."

Laying down the rod which was already somewhat frayed from Marion's energetic application of the red-head's voluptuous bare bottom, I squatted down and applied my hands to the flouncy rosette on Kay's left thigh, then tugged it down to her ankle.

"Oh, don't—oh, sir, don't shame me any more. Oh, please, it's dreadful for me to be like this in front of you—oh, do have mercy, I'll be ever so good—I apologize, truly I do, but spare me any more, let me go now!" she sobbed, heartrendingly.

I did not let myself be softened by this plaint, but now rolled down the stocking, disclosing the admirable and creamy-sheened contours of as delightfully dimpled a knee and as temptingly curved a calf as a warm-blooded man might ever hope to behold at such close proximity.

Now I began to palpate that enchanting calf and knee with lingering touches, which made the frantic, naked victim struggle afresh with her bonds as she desperately strove to clench her legs and dissemble to some extent, though she could not entirely hide it, the thickly furred gap between her naked legs. I now proceeded to the other stocking and garter and had them down in a trice, and then I slipped off her shoes; at first she tried to plant her feet solidly on the floor to prevent this, but a slight pinch to each calf drew a cry and an involuntary movement of her imprisoned legs so that I was able to divest her of her footgear. This done, it was a simple matter to take stocking and garter completely off each leg, and now Kay was clad only in her blushes, a true daughter of Eve.

"Now I think we are ready to proceed with this part of your correction, my girl," I told her as I retrieved the brich and stood before her switching it about in the air and watching with sly amusement at the terrified way her tear-blurred, hugely dilated eyes shifted hither and yon to follow its menacing flourishes.

"Oh, don't—oh, please, no more! I can't stand it! Oh, sir, what must I do to entreat you? I swear before my mistress, truly I do, I shan't ever give offense again! Oh, do have mercy now and let me go!" she babbled.

I stepped back a little to get the proper range and extended the birch till its flexible tips brushed her left leg just above the knee and to the inside.

"Let us see how sensitive it is *there*," I remarked aloud, and drawing back my hand, I inflicted a whisking cut which sent the tips over the back of her lower thigh.

"Eeéeouuuuuuul! Oh, dear Lord, I can't endure it, it's terrible! Oh, sir, Mr. Jack, do spare me, it hurts as much as on my poor b-b-bottom!" she wailed.

"I am encouraged to hear you say as much," was my cynical rejoinder, "for after your insistence that your backside was cut to ribbons when there was hardly a scratch showing, I was beginning to think you were thickskinned everywhere," and with this, patting the other jerking, creamy leg in the same manner and in the same place, I regaled it with a similar deft whisk, producing a frantic plunging and twisting about which made her bubbies jiggle in the most appetizing manner and tore a shrill plaint from her trembling lips.

"Perhaps a little higher up will be still more effective," I commented as I pressed the tips of the withes about midway up on the inside of her left thigh.

She was trembling violently now as she stared down at

196

the switches, and the muscles of her legs flexed supremely as she strove without avail to close them.

"Oh, Mr. Jack, oh heavens, not there—you'll kill me—you'll kill me! Oh sir, I beg you, I pray you, I entreat you most humbly, do spare me and forgive me! I'll do anything you order, I swear I will, if you'll only put down that dreadful rod!"

"I shall put it down when you have had your punishment in full and not before, so you might as well steel yourself and make up your mind to endure what you have so justly merited," I pronounced.

Thereupon, I cut at her inner thigh with a dextrous movement of my wrist and Kay flung back her head and shrieked with pain as the lashes curled eagerly over the tender, sensitive column her bottom plunging from side to side, and of course affording me the greatest visual pleasure as her cunt gaped and even exposed exquisite glimpses of the soft, twitching pink lips through the dark-red foliage.

Now I patted the other leg at the same place halfway up the slender, creamy thigh and tears ran down Kay's cheeks as she pitifully besought me to grant her mercy from the burning slashes. By now, as you can guess, my own rod was in a ferocious state of readiness, and I would as soon apply one as the other because the voluptuous nakedness of this dashingly handsome pert little minx whetted all my carnal appetites.

"Let us see if the birch will not be even more efficacious somewhat higher up," I ruminated, and poor Kay, whimpering and sobbing, flung herself about in every which way to escape its searching quest, which ended when the tips of the withes pressed home against her left inner thigh just below that exquisite juncture of her furry crotch.

"Oh, not there—for God's sake, not there, I beg you

197

humbly!" poor Kay pleaded, but I was adamant, and rod swept over the designated spot, producing an even more frantic twisting and a piercing yell of intolerable anguish.

Nothing daunted, I transferred the swishy rod to the other thigh just below her cunt, and after I savored her tearful and hysterical supplications to be let off, applied a stinging slash.

Marion had followed all this scene with the greatest interest, and from the panting of her magnificent bubbies and the spiteful glow in her great blue eyes, as well as from the tell-tale sign of her soft pink tongue creeping about the corners of her rosy mouth, I knew that this once haughty and aloof sister of my beloved Alice fully shared my own sadistically erotic impulses towards the redhaired captive.

For now she exhorted me, "Don't spare the naughty minx, Jack dear! Birch her well! Why, all this fuss over a few mild cuts, you'd think she was being flayed alive."

At this, Kay turned her face and piteously sobbed, "Only a few cuts? Oh my Lord, ma'am, I only wish you had to bear as many. You'd be begging mercy just as I am. Oh, how can you be so heartless to me?"

Now for me the time had come to substitute rods, as it were, for my prick would have no more of this sublimation, however exciting. And so, lowering the rod for a moment to give Kay a brief respite, I proceeded without warning to lift it till the tips of the switches pressed home against her furry cunt.

"Ooooh—noooo! For God's sake, not there! You'll kill me! Oh, Mr. Jack, for God's sake, don't whip me there!"

Her voice was wildly strident as she strained herself, as if wishing to lift herself up from the firmament and away from the deadly menace of the birch. I kept patting her cunt with the tip of the birches all this time, to impinge upon her more firmly the utter hopelessness of her situation, and then I sternly demanded, "Your spiteful tongue and your insolence have really not earned you any leniency Kay. So you must think of something better than words to appease my determination for evening our score. If you cannot, I fear you must be content with enduring your punishment till it pleases me to suspend it."

Thus intimating to her that I would consider her plea to be had instead of birched, I lowered the rod slowly, whilst her horrified and tear-drowned eyes wildly followed its peregrinations. Just as my wrist was about to flick upwards and deliver the diabolical sting into her tenderest gape, she shrieked, "Oh, don't! I'll do whatever you want—anything. Only for God's sake, ma'am, don't let him hit me there—not between the legs—oh, for God's sake, don't!"

"You must address your supplications to me now, not your mistress, since this portion of your chastisement concerns only the two of us," I interrupted. "For that further insolence, you shall have an extra three cuts in the same place after you have had your dozen."

"Ohh, my God, not so many—oh, not between the legs—wait—please don't whip me there—yes, I'll beg you—anything you want—oh, please, not between the legs—good heavens, you'll kill a girl there—mercy, mercy, Mr. Jack!" she wildly babbled.

"You must be more explicit than that," I told her as I feigned lifting the rod up towards her vulnerable Mount of Venus. Her body writhed and shrank, twisting frenziedly, as she shrieked,

"Oh, Mr. Jack, have me, do me, then, but for God's sake put down that dreadful rod!"

"Why the sinful baggage," Marion now played her role as my assistant even more delightfully than I could have hoped for even if I had coached her in advance.

"Such presumptuousness, to offer herself so shamelessly and in my presence! She deserves no mercy, Jack, and if you are softhearted enough to spare her, I shall attend to her myself when we get home."

"Oh no, no, ma'am. You don't understand—I can't bear such pain. It will kill me, surely it will. Oh, he'll let me off if I let him have me, and I can't stand it—I must—oh, please, ma'am, say you understand and forgive me that I can't endure such torture," Kay sobbed wildly. She turned her face imploringly over her shoulder towards her mistress.

"I think, Marion," I said with false gentleness, for my voice was trembling already with desire, "that she has learned her lesson. I would put her on probation. Of course, a strict probation, with the understanding that if she once more offends you, her punishment will be even more severe. Won't you excuse her from further birching this evening, now that she has shown herself to be humble and contrite?"

"Oh, very well. But all the same, the naughty hussy is getting off far too easily."

I now turned my attentions to the sobbing redhead, who hung there in her bonds, exhausted and weeping, utterly distraught.

"Do I understand you fully, my girl?" I said. "In return for my sparing you any more cuts of the rod, you wish me to have you? You are aware, I take it, what such an offer implies."

"Oh, yes! Do it and end my suffering. Do it!" she moaned.

"I had thought you much more chaste than this," was my ironic comment. "Can it be that you are not the vaunted virgin your mistess and I believed you to be? Let us find out."

With this, standing close to her, I put my hand lightly

over the huddling, birch-warmed cheeks of her naked backside, and with my right forefinger probed between the twitching outer lips of Kay's cunt. She moaned and turned her face away, tears running down her face, as I pursued my inspection. Once past the inner lips which guarded the citadel of her love channel, I felt not the least obstruction, and this I announced to Marion.

"Why, she is not at all a virgin, my finger tells me!"

"You wanton little trollop!" Marion denounced her. "How comes this loss of virtue? Was it in my service? Answer, or I shall have Mr. Jack take the birch to you again, and it would be appropriate for him to punish you in the very place with which you have offended."

I sent Marion a look of boundless admiration; she was a woman after my own heart, and it had come intuitively to her exactly how to speak and act during this voluptuous chastisement of her beautiful maid.

"Oh, I—I couldn't help it, ma'am, truly I couldn't." Kay was crying like a naughty child who has been found out.

My forefinger remained in the depths of her cunny all the while, enjoying the most delicious sensations of her palpitations.

"He—he made me, ma'am. I couldn't help myself, truly I couldn't."

"Who made you?" Marion demanded.

"Oh, don't make me tell, please don't!"

"I will cut the skin off your big backside, miss, if you don't speak," her mistress spiritedly rejoined.

"It was your—your h-husband, ma'am," Kay groaned in a dying voice.

"Oh, the ignoble wretch! And then you had the gall to reproach me for not being a proper wife to that scoundrel," Marion burst out enraged.

"Oh, forgive me, do forgive me, I'm so ashamed! Oh, have mercy!" Kay sobbed.

"I think we have had the truth at last, Marion," I interposed. "And as I told you before, this dolt of a husband of yours was the chief protagonist of all your unhappiness. You are well rid of him. So this afternoon has not been without accomplishment, for I daresay you will bring home with you a wiser and more discreet servant —isn't that so, my girl?"

"Oh y-y-yes, sir, she will never have reason to complain of me again. Please, won't you untie me now? My b-b-bottom burns me so I can hardly stand it."

"You are forgetting your generous offer to me a moment ago, which I am resolved to take advantage of," I twitted her.

Unbuttoning my trousers, I liberated my massively swollen cock and stepped forward to service the delicious, naked redhead. I circled her quivering, creamy supple waist with my left arm, so she could not pull away, and then, using right thumb and forefinger, yawned apart the portals of her slit and introduced the tip of my bulging cock between them. Kay moaned and closed her eyes, as a long tremor swept her helpless frenzied urge to emit the fearful burden weighing on my balls, I penetrated the sweet baggage.

Kay's cunt was gloriously tight—yes, as tight as her mistress's and it was evident that even if Marion's errant and boorish husband had taken her prize, he had not thoroughly acquainted her with the delicious art of fucking, for she gasped and wriggled like a true virgin when she felt my spear impale her to the hilt.

I lifted my hands to cup her bubbies now, and to revel in their springy feel to my fingers, as I stood up against her, buried in her tight warm cunt, feeling the indescribably thrilling pulsations of that vaginal sheath which so snugly housed my rampant rod.

Suddenly Kay jerked and uttered a scream, turning her face back over her shoulders. Marion had taken up the birch, and resuming her stance behind her maid, laid a bold stripe across Kay's already furiously striped hind quarters.

"Owwl Oh no, ma'am, please no more! I'm doing what he wants—you know I have to! Aiii—oh, sir, have her stop—I'm dying—oh, Lord, it's too much," Kay wailed as a second stroke of the rod danced over her shuddering hind quarters.

I was speechless with delight, for Marion had a flash of inspiration to furnish me with this memorable episode of whip-fucking. I had only to stand firmly and to cup Kay's heaving bubbies, while under Marion's inspired cuts, the naked captive procured for me the maximum of sensations in her sporadic heavings and wrigglings; and in her frenzied gyrations each time the birch cut across her backside, her weavings, she directed upon my aching cock the most exciting of frictional caresses, so it was not long before I uttered a cry and, digging my fingers into those welted nether globes of hers, spared her further damage by the birch as I deluged her warm tract with a bubbling drench of spunk.

Chapter 16

When at last I emerged my limpened weapon from Kay's dripping, contracting lovesheath, the lovely red-head hung in her bonds, violently shuddering in aftermath. The birching had drawn her very near to climax, as I could tell by the significant flexions of her naked, long, creamy thighs and the moans and sighings which made her beautiful, perky bubbies rise and fall with the most desultory of rhythms.

"I rather think we may now extend the laurel wreath of forgiveness to this naughty girl," I said languidly to my beautiful brunette mistress, "and in token of this new enlightened state of harmony which I trust will exist between you two henceforth, it is only meet that you give her the kiss of peace and bring her to pleasure."

"Why, whatever do you mean, dear Jack?" Marion enthusiastically demanded as she came to stand beside me and to stare greedily at the quivering nakedness of her servant.

I whispered into Marion's ear, and she gasped and blushed, flashing me a dewy look which bespoke a considerable lascivious eagerness.

"Oh, I should never dare," she whispered, but her eyes were dancing to belie that negation.

I took my handkerchief out and mopped Kay's cunt, at which the naked sufferer squirmed and moaned and wriggled again, obviously just on the verge of the appeasement which the whipping and the fucking had procured.

"It will bind the two of you closer together, Marion," I hinted, "and this evening you may discover though no husband is on hand to grace and warm your bed, your maid will be only too eager to render you sweet service."

Marion gasped, as her eyes widened. Then with a soft, husky giggle, she murmured, "What a naughty idea! Well, Kay, if I forgive you and leave it up to you, will you promise faithfully to be a good servant to me?"

"Oh, yes. Truly I will. You have only to ask and I will obey you! Oh—ma'am—what are you doing to me? Ooooaaaahhh—oh, ma'am, that t-tickles so—oh, you-u-u-u—Ohhh—I'm going to faint—Aaaaahhheeeeeoooouu-uu!!!"

For Marion, kneeling down, her fingers squeezing her maid's birch-welted bottomcheeks, had delicately applied a tender kiss on that soft cunt, and, becoming emboldened by this first essay, as well as by my whispered instructions to her now, foraged out her nimble tongue and began to gamahuch the lovely redhaired sufferer. Kay's eyes rolled in their sockets, her head turned restlessly from side to side, her fingers opened and clenched in her palms, as long, shuddering spasms rippled through her tethered body, till at last her moans and sobs and cries mounted to paroxysm as she suddenly achieved the explosive fury of her orgasm, and slumped in her bonds, her eyes closed, her bubbies heaving wildly.

Together Marion and I released Kay from the ropes, and I carried her over to the couch, while Marion hastened to fetch a glass of restorative brandy, which, kneeling solicitously before the couch, she proffered to Kay's trembling lips, her left arm under the girl's trembling shoulders. It was really a delicious tableau, and after Kay had sipped the restorative, color came back into her cheeks. Putting down the glass, Marion suddenly and impulsively leaned forward and kissed her maid passionately on the mouth, while her hand roamed down Kay's quivering belly.

"Oh, you darling, you're so lovely," she breathed, "I'm so sorry I birched you, dear! Will you forgive me and be a good girl now?"

Oh, miracle of conversion, brought about by the most honest instincts which in our flesh have the power to overcome sanctimoniousness and prudery! For the charming redhead, with a little flurried cry, flung her arms around Marion and returned her kiss with gusto as she panted, "Oh, ma'am, oh yes, of course I'll forgive you! I was wicked, and I deserved it, I know I did! I'll be such a good maid from now on, you'll never even have to scold me again, I promise."

Discreetly I determined to withdraw from this tender scene of reconciliation, but not until I had whispered in Marion's ear that she should profit from her maid's newly acquired contrition by making love to her, and indeed, in my absence, Kay might be the means to sweet erotic fulfillment for her. I then left the Snuggery and, after a quick and refreshing tub, clad myself in my silk dressing gown and sandals, and repaired back to my favorite lair, bringing with me two glasses of strong cordial. There, a breathtaking spectacle awaited me, for Marion had undressed except for hose and rosette garters, and she and Kay were lying entwined on my couch, whispering sweet nothings in each other's ears, while their lips met and their hands ardently fondled quivering contours.

"Now this delights me," I exclaimed, "for I perceive a happy augury of the future, and a bond of harmony between you both which will compensate Marion for her

206

loss of a husband. And for you, Kay, this show of sweet humility to gain reconciliation with your mistress justifies my severity with you. It remains only for you, my girl, to acknowledge that you bear me no rancor for having inflicted it."

"Oh, n . . . no . . . s . . . sir," the copperyhaired maid quavered, huddling tightly up against my naked sister-in-law to be, and her face was fiery with demure blushes as she observed that my eyes were fasting on her splendid supple nakedness. The marks of her chastisement made her finely grained pale-sheened skin especially appetizing, and I confess that my cock was rampant in tribute to such elegance of feminine proportions as she exhibited. Moreover, the dark upholstery of the couch and the decor of the cushions intensified that fairness of epidermis, while for Marion's olive-tinted skin it gave my former brunette adversary a most thrillingly exotic enhancement. Yes, as I stared at my couch in the Snuggery, I could tell myself that were I to carry out my sudden impulsive decision to wed my beloved Alice, I should have at the start of my farewell to bachelorhood such a harem as even an Oriental potentate could not surpass—perchance in quantity, yes, but not at all in quality! There would be Alice and the darkhaired Fanny as her sweetly complaisant serving-wench and in her own right as lascivious an odalisque as any virile emir or sultan could command; and then these two, and blond Connie Blunt . . .

You cannot imagine what euphoria was in my heart—and what aching joy throbbed in my cock—at this happy speculation. But now the time had come to benefit for my own part—and, speaking literally, my most concerned and ardent part!—on the healing of the rift between Marion and her rebellious baggage of a redhaired maid.

"And I take it you have quite forgiven Kay her naughtiness towards you, "I addressed the charming brunette.

"To be sure, Jack dear, and I owe it all to you. And, while you were out procuring those welcome glasses of fortifying refreshment, she gave me to understand how my wretched scoundrel of a husband not only forced her to yield to him but also constrained her to believe I was unfaithful to him and hence to spy on me for the purpose of reporting back to him so he might have a pretext to carry on his many infidelities without the stab of conscience," Marion exclaimed, the while she fondled Kay's sweet bubbies with both slim hands. "Ah, and to think, sir, that if I had not conspired with you to punish this sweet child, we should never have learned the truth! For, to be sure, you heartless rogue you, I was not at all unfaithful to Harry—nor to myself till that other afternoon when you took your revenge of my helpless person."

I bent to kiss her, and the folds of my dressing gown, at this point, slyly abetted my desire to supplement my pleasure on this memorable afternoon; for, yawning, they disclosed the renewed structure of my cock, and Kay's eyes widened as she saw the swollen red arrow-tip so close to her own blushing cheek.

"Perhaps, in the true spirit of conciliation as of strict justice, then," I said to the sleek brunette sister of my beloved Alice, "it would be only right if Kay were to chastise you for the unfounded mistrust which you had of her all this while."

At this, Kay's eyes widened still more, and then she cast her mistress a quizzical look which, I swear, was almost one of appraisal as to how it would really be to turn the tables and give back as good as she had just got.

"Now wait a bit, Jack," Marion protested, while she blushed to her temples, "I do not follow your reasoning in this. For did I not tell you that Kay was impertinent, and that is not permissible in a well-trained domestic no matter what her secret purpose may be. Moreover, this very afternoon, did she not treat you with such insolence as a fine lady might behave towards her social equal? And that too is decidedly unpardonable."

"Granted," I chuckled amiably, "but let me remind you that I have already paid Kay back in full for her untoward conduct towards me, as she herself will doubtless testify."

"Oh, indeed you did, Mr. Jack," Kay ruefully gasped, as she slipped one dainty hand towards her well-marked naked backside, "and I can still feel those dreadful stinging cuts on my tender bum."

"Very well, Marion, you are answered, and my sentence is this: to effect the fullest reconciliation between yourself and Kay, you shall submit to a good bottom-smacking at her fair hand, after which the both of you will kiss and make up and avow that henceforth you will be not only mistress and maid but the closest of friends and confidantes!"

"Oh yes, Mr. Jack!" Kay now eagerly broke in, "I confess I've always longed to chastise Miss Marion, the overbearing way she acted to me when I was but a poor novice in her service and already under Mr. Harry's stern orders to obey him implicitly and not to defer to her. I do so want to smack her lovely bum, I do for a fact, sir!"

Marion gasped and tried to rise from the couch, but now, since it was only fair to give tit for tat, I seated myself at one end and seized her by the wrists and drew her over my lap in the classical attitude of a naughty child readied for chastisement. "Oh, no, Jack, you—oh, you're embarrassing me dreadfully," Marion panted, wriggling and trying to twist off my lap. But I would have none of it and, shifting her svelte naked body made her kicking stockinged long legs angle down to the floor, whereupon I promptly clamped my right leg over her calves to pinion her effectively, whilst my right arm circled her slim waist and with my left hand I grasped her right wrist and drew it up against my body, this completely subjugating her. Though her left arm was free, she could not conveniently reach back down to cover up the upturned olive-satiny cheeks of her magnificent posterior, and the stage was set for this delightful reversal of relationship between once equally arrogant mistress and supercilious, disapproving domestic in which I had played the role of the equitable Solomon.

"Now then, Kay," I instructed the sparkling-eyed copperyhaired minx, who had risen and come over to my end of the couch to watch my subjugation of her beautiful naked mistress, "smack your mistress's backside soundly, but do not hurry the smacks. Let each have ample time to register its biting sting, so that she will feel the weight of your little hand. I shall determine when thorough justice has been rendered."

"Oh, you heartless creature, you have trapped me," Marion indignantly protested and tried her best to struggle, arching and twisting her magnificent bare bottom, trying to reach my pinioning hand with her free one. But I leaned to her and commanded, "Resign yourself, dear Marion, or I will have Kay use a birch instead of her hand on your saucy backside!" which quite made her subside. Hanging her head and closing her eyes, as her cheeks reddened in shame, she prepared herself to receive this juvenile chastisement, which surely must have numiliated her, especially in my presence.

Kay leaned over, thereby providng me witn the mouthwatering sight of those two lovely naked bubbies of hers dangling like the fruits with which poor Tantalus was tortured by the malicious rulers of Mount Olympus,

and she seemed to be scrutininizing the flinching, huddling firm, resilient olive-satiny cheeks of Marion's behind with a view towards determing where it would
cause her mistress the most discomfort to strike.

Then at last she raised her right hand and brought it
down with a lovely, noisy "Smack!" solidly on the right
summit of Marion's velvety behind, leaving a bright pink
imprint of her palm and causing my helpless naked
brunette captive to tense herself and utter a stifled gasp
which indicated that she had felt the chastening sting.

I could see from the delighted expression on the redhaired baggage's face that she had just discovered a vast-
ly amusing pastime. "Very good," I commended her, "but
conserve your strength, or after only a few sound smacks
you will find yourself not only tiring but suffering nearly
as much as your charming patient. Carefully dosed and
gradually increasing severity is the secret of this juvenile chastisement."

"Yes, Mr. Jack, I see," Kay murmured, pursing her lips
thoughtfully as if I had just diaphanously explained Mr.
Gladstone's position on the British colonial policy. Raising her hand, she applied the second spank on the other
cheek of Marion's squirming backside, not quite so vehe-
mently, but, I assure you, sufficiently to cause the brunette to gasp again and to try to kick up her pinioned
stockinged legs which my right leg still efficaciously imprisoned.

"That is the way, and now that you have discovered it,
proceed at your leisure," I remarked, whilst Marion indignantly turning her flushed face back to me, exclaimed, "This is not fair of you, Jack, to traitorously en-
courage the girl to make my ordeal one of scientific torture!"

"Will you confess yourself less stoic than your maid
who bore a goodly number of severe cuts with the birch

over her tender posterior?" I taunted Marion, who at once bit her lips, turned away her head and steeled herself to evince her Spartan fortitude.

But Kay took this as a challenge to her own newly found fustigatory powers, and proceeded to smack her mistress's squirming upturned bottom quite vigorously, distributing the slaps equitably over both tensing, huddling, then relaxing, globes till the warm olive hue of Marion's smooth epidermis turned from bright pink to vivid crimson and till my brunette sister-in-law to be began to lift her head and stare with dilated, humid eyes out ahead of her, while her free hand clenched and thrust against the back of the couch to distract herself from the cumulative warmth and sting which Kay's hand was imparting to her naked behind. I watched with gloating pleasure at the exquisite vision of Marion's stockinged thighs flexing and squirming, of the long rippling tremors that passed from the bare flesh of her upper thighs over the beleaguered globes of her naked seat, to pass along the lovely hollowed column of her naked back. Now, from about the fifteenth smack on, Marion announced the reception of Kay's flattening palm on her resilient flesh with a nervous, flurried gasp, and when her maid, after pausing at what I counted to be about the twenty-fifth or twenty-sixth, blew on her palm, then lifted it and brought it down with redoubled energy to flatten the inner curves of both naked, reddening globes, she uttered a sobbing "Ahhh! Oh, that's enough now, Jack, make her stop, it's becoming painful to me!"

But I had no such intention. I wished Marion's erotic senses to be roused by this voluptuous correction, which, as I could clearly see from the look on Kay's flushed, vivacious face and the panting swell of her beautiful naked bubbies, was having a similar effect on the maid's warm temperament. So I jestingly countered, "I had believed

212

you to be a mature woman, my dear, but here you are complaining over a childish smackbottom which would not bring tears to the eyes of a twelve-year-old boarding-school pupil!"

"Oh, Mr. Jack, my hand is beginning to smart from her big backside, "Kay now saucily profferred, "might I not try a birch on her for a change?"

"Oh, no, don't let her birch me, for Lord's sake, Jack dear," Marion now really became alarmed as she struggled to get loose, wearing her flaming bottom in the most salacious manner. By now, needless to remark, my cock was frantically roused by all her squirmings over it, and, shifting her a bit as I signed for Kay to wait, I drew aside the folds of my dressing gown so that my fulminating weapon might be free to profess its ardor by rubbing against Marion's belly and loins while she struggled under the smackbottom Kay was so ably administering.

"To rest your smarting palm a moment, Kay," I advised, "try to let your hand act as a whip. Thusly, let your fingers be limp and loose and, as you bring down your hand, let them fall like the thongs of such an instrument. The flicking sting they will thus impart over a terrain so ably prepared and sensitized will, I assure you, make up for the loss of impacting force!"

"Oh, yes, I see, Mr. Jack," Kay delightedly cried. Now she knelt down on the floor, and, lifting her right hand slowly aloft, whisked it down exactly as I had instructed, the tips of her fingers nipping the base of Marion's right buttock.

"Ooooh, ohh, please!" Marion tearfully exclaimed as her hips swerved from side to side, "do make her stop! I hate you for being so cruel!"

"But if you only realized that a man must be cruel to be kind, my dear, you would be more appreciative of this."

213

"You in turn, my girl," addressing myself to the charming, kneeling, naked redhaired minx, "must reciprocate in the loveliest way two females can demonstrate their amity for each other."

With this, I unclamped my leg over Marion's, and, releasing her captive wrist, took hold of her hips with both hands, gesturing to Kay to lift her by the wrists, and thus the brunette was drawn to her feet, tears staining her flushed cheeks and her magnificent bubbies in tumultuous upheaval. "Now, then, clasp each other in each other's arms, and kiss sweetly," I ordered, and was obeyed. To see these two delicious females clad only in their hose and rosette garters standing, their naked bodies merged, their breasts mashing together, their mouths joined, and to observe the welts and scratches on Kay's voluptuous dreamy backside from the birching and on Marion's once olive-hued posterior the fiery red of that admirable bottomsmacking, was to see in my mind's eye the commencement of my true harem which should be prodigiously expanded when I announced to Alice my eagerness to explore nuptual bliss with her delightful person. I stood a moment in rapt contemplation of the gracious Sapphic unison of these two beauties, till the adamant compulsion of my own needs roused me to proceed with the last part of the afternoon's program.

Chapter 17

They had begun to murmur solicitous words, apologetic and compassionate, each imploring the other's pardon for having inflicted suffering on her. Marion's hands had begun to caress Kay's striated naked behind, whilst Kay's slim fingers caressingly palpated her mistress's inflamed seat. They were, in a word, at the threshold of a carnal communion that would still more tangibly alter their psyches to my own amorous advantage. And that was why I now remarked, "Now this is praiseworthy, but it is not yet the generous, warmhearted unanimity I wish you both to discover for yourselves."

Questioningly, they turned their heads to regard me, then blushed to realize how naughtily wanton they were in embracing naked before a man. But the humid eyes, the moist quivering red lips, the panting globes of their beautiful naked bosoms were telltale signs that Marion were erotically stirred to the point that they could find solace in each other. And just as Fanny and Alice had "made up," so too did I wish the brunette and her red-haired minx of a servant to become amorously entwined.

"Marion, do you not find Kay charmingly made?" I asked.

"Oh, yes, Jack, she—she's so delicious, such an exquisite figure, and such fine white skin, I feel ashamed of myself for having marked it so cruelly," Marion declared.

"And you, Kay, do you not find your mistress's body to be exciting, now you've seen it unveiled and quivering under your spanking hand?" I twitted the redhead.

She blushed scarlet, lowering her eyes as she stammered, "Oh, y—yes, Mr. J—Jack, s—sir, she is really beautiful."

"There, now, you see, my dears?" I chuckled in rare good humor, "it remains for you to express that admiration in a loving way, one which we men can't, alas, emulate because of the hard difference in our sex." My audacious pun was, I fear, overlooked by both blushing naked houris, for they stared at me, not quite knowing what I was driving at.

"I will show you, then,". I said, once again summoning all my powers of self-control. "Marion, do you lie down on the couch, like a goddess who disposes herself to receive adoration from her followers."

Wonderingly, Marion walked to the couch and sank down on it, not without wincing and uttering a stifled little "Owwl!" at which I could not hold back a chuckle, in which Kay contagiously joined with a hearty giggle. But before the mood could be broken, I hurriedly instructed the saucy redhaired baggage "And now, Kay, lie down over your mistress in reverse, so that your face is over her lovely warm cunt, whilst yours is tendered to her warm sweet mouth. And thus you will give each other the true kiss of peace!"

"Ohh, Jack—that—that's terribly naughty," Marion gasped, turning scarlet to her ears, and starting to rise.

"It will be naughtier still, I fear, if you do not comply with my request, for then I shall spreadeagle you on the couch and let Kay use a feather as well as her lips and tongue on you, with the order to bring you almost to the threshold of pleasure but not to let you enter its domain," I threatened.

216

Blushingly Kay now took her position over her mistress in the figure of *soixante-neuf*, and I whispered to her that she should have two gold guineas from me if she took the initiative over her mistress. This she did by slipping her hands under Marion's bottom, and, putting her mouth to the raven thicket of her mistress's Venus mound, applied a long, sweet sucking kiss.

"Ooooh, Kay, ohh, what are you doing—ooooh!" Marion squealed, and I whispered to her, "Pay her back in kind, the wicked minx, and make her wail for mercy."

Which she at once proceeded to do. And there I stood, entranced, as these two naked beauties gamahuched each other, moaning and sighing like two nymphs of the court of sweet Bilitis herself.

But when I perceived that Kay's hips and loins had begun to wriggle and lunge, and when I heard her inarticulate sighs and groans and knew her to be further along the pathway to paradise, I flung off my dressing gown and, seizing her by the waist, lifted her off Marion's wriggling naked body and, pressing her down on her back on the rug inserted my near-bursting cock into her moist slit and with a single mighty lunge thrust myself home to the hilt.

Kay uttered a strident cry, flung her arms round my shoulders and, nimbly wrapping her stockinged legs over my sinewy and jerking behind, arched up to meet me in the frenetic gymnastics by which we both attained our approaching climax—she, because chastising Marion and then being gamahuched by her erstwhile love-victim had titillated her to unleashed passion. I because my voyeuristic pleasures had proved as violently aphrodisiacal as fucking itself!

Happily, as I had poured forth such a deluge of essence in Kay's cunt immediately after her fustigation, I discovered that my cock retained its rigidity even after it

217

had ebbed forth a token residue to acclaim the heated reception the redhaired maid's quaking love-canal had bestowed upon it. I therefore drew out and made directly from the couch, where Marion lay unrequited, moaning feverishly, one slim hand now slyly frigging herself as she posed with heels planted on the couch, knees up and yawningly straddled. And I chided her teasingly. "I will give that little hand something better to play with. Reach out and guide it!"

Whereupon, opening her humid eyes, and uttering a joyous gasp of "Ohh, yes, Jack dearest, oh that'll be ever so much better," Marion grasped my ramrod and drew it to her twitching moist pink crevice. And once again with a single mighty lunge, I impaled her to my very balls. Then began to fuck her with long hard digs, while she clutched me with arms and stockinged legs, moaning and kissing me feverishly, till she gave down her furious tribute.

Gallantly, I then retired, to let the ladies enjoy the privacy of the bidet and W.C. at the back of the Snuggery, whilst I repaired to my own private place to make my ablutions and to put on a new dressing gown. When I returned, to my secret amusement, I found Marion and Kay seated side by side on the couch, still naked save for their hose, cuddling and whispering to each other like old friends.

And when at last they dressed and took their leave of me, Marion kissed me, saying, "How lovely this has been, dear Jack, and how grateful Kay and I must be to you, for bringing us together."

"Then I'm forgiven and there's no longer war between us, Marion?" I laughed.

She shook her head, blushed, and squeezed Kay's hand.

"Bravo, my dear! And may I dare to hope that you will

218

favor me with a visit in future—and bring your lovely maid, perhaps, too?" I hazarded.

"Oh, yes, yes, do please, Miss Marion, ma'am," Kay exclaimed and then turned away her blushing face.

"Why you forward minx," Marion laughed goodnaturedly, "that will depend on your good conduct henceforth." Then, to me, she murmured, with a bewitched *moué*. "It seems we shall be related, sir, if you mean to keep your word concerning Alice."

"And so I do. When she returns next week, I mean to propose the honorable estate of marriage to her, if she'll have me."

"Oh, she will, if she knows what's good for her, the minx," Marion rather sulkily murmured. And then, flirtatiously, in a husky, intimate tone that made me quiver with anticipation of the future, "But if she doesn't, then perhaps I will, sir."

And on this fortuitous note, we parted, enemies no more, but the most intimate of friends, if that sweet amity which exists between man and maid may be called by so pallid a term.

Yes, at last I had had my revenge on haughty Marion. And I had discovered beneath her arrogant veneer the temperament of the most ardent of mistresses. How I wooed her sister and came to the ceremonial for formal nuptuals which I am frank to admit, I had not previously contemplated, is another story—as is that of the realization of my dream of a "harem" which would not only include the quartet of two sisters and their amorous maids but also the beauteous young widow Connie Blunt and other as yet unknown warm-blooded damsels. And perhaps, dear reader, one day I shall record it with the heartfelt wish that it will let you glean a small part of the enjoyment, nay, the ecstasy, that was mine!

THE BEST IN EROTIC READING – BY POST

The Nexus Library of Erotica – almost one hundred and fifty volumes – is available from many booksellers and newsagents. If you have any difficulty obtaining the books you require, you can order them by post. Photocopy the list below, or tear the list out of the book; then tick the titles you want and fill in the form at the end of the list. Titles marked 1993 are not yet available: please do not try to order them – just look out for them in the shops!

CONTEMPORARY EROTICA

AMAZONS	Erin Caine	£3.99	
COCKTAILS	Stanley Carten	£3.99	
CITY OF ONE-NIGHT STANDS	Stanley Carten	£4.50	
CONTOURS OF DARKNESS	Marco Vassi	£4.99	
THE GENTLE DEGENERATES	Marco Vassi	£4.99	
MIND BLOWER	Marco Vassi	£4.99	
THE SALINE SOLUTION	Marco Vassi	£4.99	
DARK FANTASIES	Nigel Anthony	£4.99	
THE DAYS AND NIGHTS OF MIGUMI	P.M.	£4.50	
THE LATIN LOVER	P.M.	£3.99	
THE DEVIL'S ADVOCATE	Anonymous	£4.50	
DIPLOMATIC SECRETS	Antoine Lelouche	£3.50	
DIPLOMATIC PLEASURES	Antoine Lelouche	£3.50	
DIPLOMATIC DIVERSIONS	Antoine Lelouche	£4.50	
ENGINE OF DESIRE	Alexis Arven	£3.99	
DIRTY WORK	Alexis Arven	£3.99	
DREAMS OF FAIR WOMEN	Celeste Arden	£2.99	
THE FANTASY HUNTERS	Celeste Arden	£3.99	
A GALLERY OF NUDES	Anthony Grey	£3.99	
THE GIRL FROM PAGE 3	Mike Angelo	£3.99	
HELEN – A MODERN ODALISQUE	James Stern	£4.99	1993
HOT HOLLYWOOD NIGHTS	Nigel Anthony	£4.50	
THE INSTITUTE	Maria del Ray	£4.99	

LAURE-ANNE	Laure-Anne	£4.50	
LAURE-ANNE ENCORE	Laure-Anne	£4.99	
LAURE-ANNE TOUJOURS	Laure-Anne	£4.99	
A MISSION FOR Ms DEEDS	Carole Andrews	£4.99	1993
Ms DEEDES AT HOME	Carole Andrews	£4.50	
Ms DEEDES ON PARADISE ISLAND	Carole Andrews	£4.99	1993
MY SEX MY SOUL	Amelia Greene	£2.99	
OBSESSION	Maria del Rey	£4.99	1993
ONE WEEK IN THE PRIVATE HOUSE	Esme Ombreux	£4.50	
PALACE OF FANTASIES	Delver Maddingley	£4.99	
PALACE OF SWEETHEARTS	Delver Maddingley	£4.99	1993
PARADISE BAY	Maria del Rey	£4.50	
QUEENIE AND CO	Francesca Jones	£4.99	1993
QUEENIE AND CO IN JAPAN	Francesca Jones	£4.99	1993
QUEENIE AND CO IN ARGENTINA	Francesca Jones	£4.99	1993
THE SECRET WEB	Jane-Anne Roberts	£3.99	
SECRETS LIE ON PILLOWS	James Arbroath	£4.50	
SECRETS IN SUMATRA	James Arbroath	£4.99	1993
STEPHANIE	Susanna Hughes	£4.50	
STEPHANIE'S CASTLE	Susanna Hughes	£4.50	
STEPHENIE'S DOMAIN	Susanna Hughes	£4.99	1993
STEPHANIE'S REVENGE	Susanna Hughes	£4.99	1993
THE DOMINO TATTOO	Cyrian Amberlake	£4.50	
THE DOMINO ENIGMA	Cyrian Amberlake	£3.99	
THE DOMINO QUEEN	Cyrian Amberlake	£4.99	

EROTIC SCIENCE FICTION

ADVENTURES IN THE PLEASURE ZONE	Delaney Silver	£4.99	
EROGINA	Christopher Denham	£4.50	
HARD DRIVE	Stanley Carten	£4.99	
PLEASUREHOUSE 13	Agnetha Anders	£3.99	
LAST DAYS OF THE PLEASUREHOUSE	Agnetha Anders	£4.50	
TO PARADISE AND BACK	D.H.Master	£4.50	
WICKED	Andrea Arven	£3.99	
WILD	Andrea Arven	£4.50	

ANCIENT & FANTASY SETTINGS

CHAMPIONS OF LOVE	Anonymous	£3.99	
CHAMPIONS OF DESIRE	Anonymous	£3.99	

CHAMPIONS OF PLEASURE	Anonymous	£3.50	
THE SLAVE OF LIDIR	Aran Ashe	£4.50	
THE FOREST OF BONDAGE	Aran Ashe	£4.50	
KNIGHTS OF PLEASURE	Erin Caine	£4.50	
PLEASURE ISLAND	Aran Ashe	£4.99	
ROMAN ORGY	Marcus van Heller	£4.50	

EDWARDIAN, VICTORIAN & OLDER EROTICA

ADVENTURES OF A SCHOOLBOY	Anonymous	£3.99	
THE AUTOBIOGRAPHY OF A FLEA	Anonymous	£2.99	
BEATRICE	Anonymous	£3.99	
THE BOUDOIR	Anonymous	£3.99	
CASTLE AMOR	Erin Caine	£4.99	1993
CHOOSING LOVERS FOR JUSTINE	Aran Ashe	£4.99	1993
THE DIARY OF A CHAMBERMAID	Mirabeau	£2.99	
THE LIFTED CURTAIN	Mirabeau	£4.99	
EVELINE	Anonymous	£2.99	
MORE EVELINE	Anonymous	£3.99	
FESTIVAL OF VENUS	Anonymous	£4.50	
'FRANK' & I	Anonymous	£2.99	
GARDENS OF DESIRE	Roger Rougiere	£4.50	
OH, WICKED COUNTRY	Anonymous	£2.99	
LASCIVIOUS SCENES	Anonymous	£4.50	
THE LASCIVIOUS MONK	Anonymous	£4.50	
LAURA MIDDLETON	Anonymous	£3.99	
A MAN WITH A MAID 1	Anonymous	£4.99	
A MAN WITH A MAID 2	Anonymous	£4.99	
A MAN WITH A MAID 3	Anonymous	£4.99	
MAUDIE	Anonymous	£2.99	
THE MEMOIRS OF DOLLY MORTON	Anonymous	£4.50	
A NIGHT IN A MOORISH HAREM	Anonymous	£3.99	
PARISIAN FROLICS	Anonymous	£2.99	
PLEASURE BOUND	Anonymous	£3.99	
THE PLEASURES OF LOLOTTE	Andrea de Nerciat	£3.99	
THE PRIMA DONNA	Anonymous	£3.99	
RANDIANA	Anonymous	£4.50	
REGINE	E.K.	£2.99	

THE ROMANCE OF LUST 1	Anonymous	£3.99	
THE ROMANCE OF LUST 2	Anonymous	£2.99	
ROSA FIELDING	Anonymous	£2.99	
SUBURBAN SOULS 1	Anonymous	£2.99	
SURBURBAN SOULS 2	Anonymous	£3.99	
THREE TIMES A WOMAN	Anonymous	£2.99	
THE TWO SISTERS	Anonymous	£3.99	
VIOLETTE	Anonymous	£4.99	

"THE JAZZ AGE"

ALTAR OF VENUS	Anonymous	£3.99	
THE SECRET GARDEN ROOM	Georgette de la Tour	£3.50	
BEHIND THE BEADED CURTAIN	Georgette de la Tour	£3.50	
BLANCHE	Anonymous	£3.99	
BLUE ANGEL NIGHTS	Margaret von Falkensee	£4.99	
BLUE ANGEL DAYS	Margaret von Falkensee	£4.99	
BLUE ANGEL SECRETS	Margaret von Falkensee	£4.99	
CAROUSEL	Anonymous	£4.50	
CONFESSIONS OF AN ENGLISH MAID	Anonymous	£3.99	
FLOSSIE	Anonymous	£2.50	
SABINE	Anonymous	£3.99	
PLAISIR D'AMOUR	Anne-Marie Villefranche	£4.50	
FOLIES D'AMOUR	Anne-Marie Villefranche	£2.99	
JOIE D'AMOUR	Anne-Marie Villefranche	£3.99	
MYSTERE D'AMOUR	Anne-Marie Villefranche	£3.99	
SECRETS D'AMOUR	Anne-Marie Villefranche	£3.50	
SOUVENIR D'AMOUR	Anne-Marie Villefranche	£3.99	

WORLD WAR 2

SPIES IN SILK	Piers Falconer	£4.50	
WAR IN HIGH HEELS	Piers Falconer	£4.99	1993

CONTEMPORARY FRENCH EROTICA (translated into English)

EXPLOITS OF A YOUNG DON JUAN	Anonymous	£2.99	
INDISCREET MEMOIRS	Alain Dorval	£2.99	
INSTRUMENT OF PLEASURE	Celeste Piano	£4.50	
JOY	Joy Laurey	£2.99	
JOY AND JOAN	Joy Laurey	£2.99	

JOY IN LOVE	Joy Laurey	£2.75	
LILIANE	Paul Verguin	£3.50	
MANDOLINE	Anonymous	£3.99	
LUST IN PARIS	Antoine S.	£4.99	
NYMPH IN PARIS	Galia S.	£2.99	
SCARLET NIGHTS	Juan Muntaner	£3.99	
SENSUAL LIAISONS	Anonymous	£3.50	
SENSUAL SECRETS	Anonymous	£3.99	
THE NEW STORY OF O	Anonymous	£4.50	
THE IMAGE	Jean de Berg	£3.99	
VIRGINIE	Nathalie Perreau	£4.50	
THE PAPER WOMAN	Francois Rey	£4.50	

SAMPLERS & COLLECTIONS

EROTICON 1	ed. J-P Spencer	£4.50	
EROTICON 2	ed. J-P Spencer	£4.50	
EROTICON 3	ed. J-P Spencer	£4.50	
EROTICON 4	ed. J-P Spencer	£4.99	
NEW EROTICA 1	ed. Esme Ombreux	£4.99	
THE FIESTA LETTERS	ed. Chris Lloyd	£4.50	
THE PLEASURES OF LOVING	ed. Maren Sell	£3.99	

NON-FICTION

HOW TO DRIVE YOUR MAN WILD IN BED	Graham Masterton	£4.50	
HOW TO DRIVE YOUR WOMAN WILD IN BED	Graham Masterton	£3.99	
HOW TO BE THE PERFECT LOVER	Graham Masterton	£2.99	
FEMALE SEXUAL AWARENESS	Barry & Emily McCarthy	£5.99	
LINZI DREW'S PLEASURE GUIDE	Linzi Drew	£4.99	
LETTERS TO LINZI	Linzi Drew	£4.99	1993
WHAT MEN WANT	Susan Crain Bakos	£3.99	
YOUR SEXUAL SECRETS	Marty Klein	£3.99	

Please send me the books I have ticked above.

Name   ....
Address   ....
           ....
           ....Post code ....

Send to: **Nexus Books Cash Sales, PO Box 11, Falmouth, Cornwall, TR10 9EN**

Please enclose a cheque or postal order, made payable to **Nexus Books**, to the value of the books you have ordered plus postage and packing costs as follows:

UK and BFPO – £1.00 for the first book, 50p for the second book, and 30p for each subsequent book to a maximum of £3.00;

Overseas (including Republic of Ireland) – £2.00 for the first book, £1.00 for the second book, and 50p for each subsequent book.

If you would prefer to pay by VISA or ACCESS/MASTERCARD, please write your card number here:

— — — —   — — — —   — — — —   — — — —

Signature: _____

Still recovering her breath after her mad dash from the hospital and the speedy change into her Christmas Fairy costume, Lara smoothed a hand over the glittering net and tulle that floated around her pink tights.

She gazed idly at the two little girls who were next in the queue. They were gorgeous. She watched them for a moment with amusement, and then looked at the father.

And froze in panic.

Oh, no, no, *no!* It was Christian Blake. Only now there was no sign of the ruthlessly efficient consultant. This afternoon he was definitely the man and not the doctor. So, he had two perfect children. And they'd picked this particular day to see Father Christmas.

The little girl who had been holding Christian's hand danced forward, her blonde curls bouncing around her face. 'Is it our turn now? Is he ready for us?'

Aggie sat next to Father Christmas, her eyes sparkling, and smiled happily. 'OK. Well, my list is just one thing—and it isn't even for me.'

Father Christmas stroked his beard. 'Who is it for, then?'

'My dad. What he needs is a miracle. I read about them in a book. A miracle is something amazing that changes everything. If I'm extra good between now and Christmas, could I have a small miracle? Daddy needs a new wife.'

Sarah Morgan trained as a nurse, and has since worked in a variety of health-related jobs. Married to a gorgeous businessman, who still makes her knees knock, she spends most of her time trying to keep up with their two little boys, but manages to sneak off occasionally to indulge her passion for writing romance. Sarah loves outdoor life, and is an enthusiastic skier and walker. Whatever she is doing, her head is always full of new characters and she is addicted to happy endings.

Recent titles by the same author:

Medical Romance™

Modern Romance™